Another Journeys

Another Butterfly

HOWCHI KILBURN

atmosphere press

Much gratitude to my sources of inspiration
especially
Jaichima, Ma'arakame (shaman/healer) of the Huichol tribe,
Riane Eisler, author of *Sacred Pleasure,*
Marija Gimbutas, author of *The Living Goddesses,*
Suzuki Roshi, Zen master,
and everyone who crusades for the good of all

Table of Contents

Prologue

They are an unlikely pair: Wu, the wandering Taoist, and Daphne, young, blond, energetic and devoted to the practice of martial arts, meditative states and other-worldly journeys. Their teacher, Grandmother Xochitl, is a medicine woman in a remote village in New Mexico devoted to the ancient traditions. Taoists, pagans and shamans engage in a sustainable way of living with lots of mystical ecstasy.

Goddess speaks to them through angels, nature spirits and the Ancient Ones, who still have enclaves in remote places on Earth. They whisper in the wind and rumble from inside the earth with voices of maternal and erotic love, while clarifying the Original Instructions given to all humans.

Shape-shifting, communion with animal and plant allies, journeys into the Spirit World and healing ceremonies are among their masteries and mysteries. It's a training program to develop skills and responsibilities, so they may play their part in the creation of a new world.

Two young people, Aiyana and Atsa, join with Wu and Daphne for the next step in their spiritual journey, a road trip across Northern New Mexico. Their destination is a community where many of Daphne and Wu's friends are living with the intention of treating this world with dedicated care and respect while cultivating relationships in conscious sisterhood and brotherhood with beings whose primary home is in other realms.

Instincts and Inclinations

*Demonstrate that people can be trusted, that the environment
can be trusted, that we live in a benign universe.*
~ Peggy O'Mara

I have begun to listen to the teaching my blood whispers to me.
~ Hermann Hesse

"I am honored to travel with you. Young people like you
are the hope of the world." Wu was amazed at how much
he was feeling just being with these three old souls.

"We know," Aiyana teased him.

"I wanted friends like you," he continued. "Are there more
like you?"

"Wu, have you been struck by thunder?" Daphne asked.

"Everything that has happened has opened me so far, I feel
inside out. I haven't been hiding from the world. I've been hiding from myself. I hope it's not too late."

"Too late how?" Aiyana queried.

"I'm old."

Quietly, Atsa offered, "You're barely an adult in my tribe.
You can probably see why."

"How did you two get so wise?"

"We hung out with the traditional elders as much as we could," Aiyana answered. "Near-death journeys can be an instant download of the truths we search for most of the time and have a hard time finding"

"That's right," Daphne declared. "We haven't heard what it was like being the focus of everyone's healing efforts and energies...if you're okay talking about it."

Atsa replied, "I can tell you a few things. I may have some individual messages for each of you. Most of what I remember I need to hold onto for a while."

The high desert of New Mexico spread out in all directions. The jeep that Atsa had borrowed was geared low and topped out around sixty. He kept it at a steady, mellow 45-50, which was only half the speed of the 90-mph world that periodically raced by them on the way to some indeterminate but apparently vital goal.

He often stopped by the side of the road or pulled onto a dirt side road, so they could wander on the land for a while. Not long after they had left, Aiyana shared with them, "Grandmother told me one thing about this journey. 'Stay connected to the land. Don't lose yourself in the traveling and forget what it's like to have your feet on the earth for days at a time with no motors, no mechanics, no electrical hum'".

Aiyana and Atsa often wandered together, becoming more and more inseparable, at least in the journey of their souls. Wu and Daphne would usually go in another direction. On the second day they came across a sidewinder near a pile of large boulders.

"Must be a snake home." Daphne pointed at the boulders. They kept their distance and were able to follow the sidewinder for several minutes before it serpentined into another collection of boulders and disappeared.

"Any messages?" Wu asked half in jest.

Daphne grinned at him. "You better watch out." She nudged him in the ribs with her elbow. "Seriously though, I have a strong sense that the snakes know we're traveling, and are protecting us along the way."

That same day Aiyana and Atsa sat for a while near a large anthill. "Can you feel how connected they are with each other? Aiyana asked.

"Yeah, how do we know that?"

"You feel it, right?"

"Yeah, but I couldn't describe to anyone who hadn't felt it."

"Direct experience. That's what Gran always says. Book learning only gets us so far."

"Right, you can't commune with the spirits by reading about how it's done. My healing could be described in a book, but it couldn't happen in a book."

"So tell me just one thing. I can't expect the whole story, but I'd love to get some little pieces.'

"Okay, when Wu was breathing into my chest, I felt warmth in my whole body, like his warm breath could fill me, and it felt wonderful...ecstatic. It's like it was a channel for everyone's love in the whole circle. I felt so loved."

"You were. You are. Do we get to hang out with your family on this trip?"

"We'll see."

"I want to know everything about you. That starts with your family."

"We have heroes and no-accounts like any family. I have aunts and uncles and cousins who are on the land with the sheep most of the time. They are very traditional. Some of them knew about Grandmother and got me to the healing ceremony. Everyone helped. Even our Christian relatives know that our ceremonies work. At least most of them do. We don't usually fight about beliefs. It's just different pathways to Spirit, different ways of communing. When someone gets healed like I did, we'll probably be drawn to hang out more with the traditional folk and the medicine people."

"Have you had other experiences like the healing ceremony?"

"I don't know what qualifies, but when I was a little kid, I often slept with the sheep. They were warm and fluffy, but probably more important, it was my first experience of feeling like a relative to a four-legged being. I felt safe and warm and loved, which might sound strange."

"Not at all. We're all part of at least one animal family, aren't we?"

Northern New Mexico, not so far from Colorado, Atsa seemed to know where he was going when he suddenly left the highway for a dirt side road that took them back to the northeast and soon entered a canyon with only a trickle of a creek, a road that was barely a trail, mostly covered by new and old weeds slowly reclaiming the land.

Atsa slowed to a halt and stated quietly, "Even a jeep's not much good from here on." As they hit the ground, he provided instructions. "Whatever you think you'll need in the next few days."

"Food?" Daphne asked.

"For sure and layers of clothing and sleeping bags or whatever for nighttime."

Wu and Daphne exchanged a glance. They spent many a night resting comfortably under one large poncho, occasionally swapping positions in their yab-yum meditation.

Soon the terrain grew steeper as they proceeded up the canyon. Atsa didn't volunteer where he was taking them, and nobody asked. With occasional breathers, they hiked that way the rest of the afternoon. Wu was struck with how green everything was within a few feet of the creek. The occasional cottonwood tree marked their progress. An uncharacteristically flat area harbored several such trees.

"We'll camp here," Atsa announced.

"Wanna tell us what's going on?" Aiyana threw out the question half as a tease.

Atsa looked at each of them for a moment. "If we're lucky, we'll have a visitor. Probably not tonight. Probably tomorrow."

Before it disappeared, the sun cast a brilliant golden glow on everything it touched. Atsa laid a small fire in preparation for the impending cool darkness. Wu and Daphne returned from an afternoon foray farther up the narrow canyon, any opportunity to practice their yab-yum meditation. The interweaving of light and shadow, opening to the fullness of the watercourse way. Their stamina was encouraged by periodically switching positions and resuming their cultivation of samadhi. They had never been naked with each other, but felt a deep understanding of each other's essential selves, an energetic awareness and intimacy. Aiyana climbed to a ledge above their campsite where she could watch Atsa as he puttered around the area, seemingly arranging things to match a picture in his mind and preparing for a visit. She loved to watch him. He had so much self-assurance since his healing ceremony, which clearly served to restore him to himself.

When he had first been brought to the village and the people gathered to care for him, he had seemed like such a misbegotten child. Without being obnoxious about it, he seemed to be rapidly growing into a role of leadership or at least the one who initiated the right thing at the right time. As she watched he would often pause as if listening, not because he'd heard something, just because it's good to make a point to consciously stop and listen periodically. "Never know when you might hear something," he sometimes quipped. He also scanned his surroundings, near and far, noting anything that was different from his last scan. He knew the message of a ground squirrel could be just as important as seeing an eagle.

Aiyana loved his attunement. "I must be falling in love," she thought. "I sure am feeling a lot that I've never felt before, including how perfect I think he is."

He had shared his nascent feelings with Grandmother Xochitl. She gazed at him with her enigmatic half-smile and simply told him, "Care for her as something really precious. Remember how young she is. You have good allies. Let them guide you."

When looking around, his gaze would rest on Aiyana for a while. He beamed to her all the love he felt and then continued his creation of ceremonial space. He was constructing a small medicine wheel from rock and branches and other found objects. From her vantage point she could clearly see the four large stones marking the cardinal directions. He was also tying objects in the cottonwood trees. She couldn't distinguish exactly what they were, but they reflected brilliant colors when they caught a glint of sunlight.

Atsa had lit the fire he'd laid earlier. Dusk was darkening as the four of them sat around the small fire. Suddenly S/he was sitting with them in their circle. None of them could have said how s/he arrived. Now the five of them sat quietly together.

As they sat in the flickering firelight, s/he gradually morphed from the extremes of masculine and feminine and everything in between the seemingly endless transition from one state of being to another. Each manifestation faded into the next, apparently without effort. S/he's beatific half-smile was the steady anchor to the change that surrounded them.

Mammoth hunter, geisha, Krishna, Kali, Great Mother, Brahma, anything and everything and then it stopped, and s/he was such an enigmatic transgender, poly-racial, Buddha and Thunder Being. S/he spoke. "What would you like to know?"

"Who are you?" Aiyana blurted.

Did S/he's smile broaden slightly? "I am everything, and I am whatever you want me to be. I am ephemeral. I have always been here and always will be."

"Are you flesh and blood, or are you pure spirit? Daphne asked.

"Yes, I pass through both of those conditions."

"Perhaps there is some purpose in all of us being together here at this time," Wu offered.

After a long silence, s/he answered. "Your openness is an opportunity for me."

"Opportunity for what?"

"To show." Long pause. "You have been chosen to receive certain understandings that have almost disappeared from Earth in this latest era."

"Do you live around here?" Aiyana asked.

"Sometimes. When the invaders came, many of us disappeared into the Other World Some of us faded into remote places and erected barriers to being seen or sensed in any way. As you know it was not safe to be native in these lands. Yet the seed of Kokopelli could not be lost. No matter how far astray; no matter how violent toward nature; no matter how estranged from spirit, there had to be a nucleus of those who knew the way back and when the time came, show others. You are already part way there. You've had experiences that transcend the contingencies of the material world."

"So now what?" Atsa spoke for the first time.

S/he floated up from where s/he sat. Then the other four were floating as well. S/he was in the center about three feet off the ground. The other four commanded the Four Directions in a perfect mandala. S/he slowly rotated as s/he spoke. "What you think of as the rules of the physical universe are only conditions augmented by beliefs. Almost everyone on

Earth has been hearing and repeating one or two limited views of what is possible for sentient beings. Imagine if you were living somewhere where what we are doing right now would be considered ordinary, just part of daily life."

"I get it," Aiyana thought. "We've all done things that most people consider impossible or crazy."

"So that's why we're here," she whispered to herself.

And S/he was saying, "First lesson: I will slowly withdraw my support of your levitation, as you take over maintaining it."

A few minutes later s/he continued. "Biological reality was supposed to be a game that we played for fun: the pleasure of eating food, running through a field of wildflowers, love and sex. Some people got so caught up in the game, they forgot it was a game. The more addicted they became, they gradually lost the ability to shape-shift out of the game, to return to the Greater Reality from which we had come.

"We did not foresee how addictive certain earthly pleasures can be. We did not understand instinct, the way it can take precedence over everything else, the thrill of the hunt, the attachment that becomes possessiveness around so-called love relationships, the tantalizing feelings elicited by certain herbs. The more attached that people became to anything in the physical realm, the more difficult it became to detach, the number one prerequisite for shape-shifting. New behaviors were invented as if one could buy insurance against the loss of precious possessions. The accumulation of wealth and power was a false promise of certainty and security, and then the attachment grew to wealth and power, not even the things that they might provide. Once accumulation is the goal, conflict is inevitable, the competition to grab whatever is available, the perception that there's not enough for everyone, the growing addiction driving a feeling that no matter how much I have, it's never enough. The mammalian brain is full of pleasures and pitfalls."

A long silence ensued. Finally Aiyana asked barely above a whisper, "Was that it?"

More silence and then S/he swept a slow circle with one arm as she rotated in place. "Now we have this world increasingly devoted to satisfying addictions and trying to assuage the fears of not having enough. You have all experienced how different, how magical things can be when we rediscover our fundamental interconnectedness. It is time."

"You must be our next guide," Daphne declared.

"I would like to travel with you for a while. I would like you to travel with me."

"Where to?"

"First, before going back to the highway, I would like you to come with me a little farther into the mountains."

Farther into the mountains always sounded good to Wu. He was the first to nod his assent, soon followed by the others.

The next morning S/he led them as far up the rocky canyon as they were able to go. As the others pondered, "What now?" they simultaneously noticed a notch in the rock wall to their left. Had it been there all the time, or had it just suddenly materialized. As they walked toward it, the notch seemed to be growing larger until they stood in front of a crack wide enough for a person to walk through. It extended through the solid rock so far that they couldn't see the other end. S/he motioned for them to follow as s/he entered the crack.

As they proceeded, the crack should have become darker, but somehow it was remaining illuminated even when they could no longer see either end. The walls were surprisingly smooth like polished agate. Eventually they got closer to a brighter light and emerged into an entirely enclosed approximate circle, perhaps a hundred yards in diameter. The walls were almost vertical and appeared pleated like curtains with the same lacy agate designs.

S/he led them to the center of the circle. "You may sit here, if you please," s/he urged. "It might be a good time to meditate. Others are with us, but you cannot see them yet."

The four sat on the smooth rock. Daphne came to Wu's lap and wrapped her legs around his torso. They were soon adrift in their well-practiced mindfulness and more. Aiyana and Atsa looked at each other. She moved him and positioned herself as Daphne was with Wu. They were soon able to relax and utilize the physical closeness as an augmentation not a distraction from deeper states of meditative awareness. The four lost track of time as they cruised in their comfortable state of be-ingness. Nothing stood out from the pearlescent silver-gray reflection of their own minds.

Aiyana was also aware of just feeling extremely comfortable and safe. Atsa marveled at how well their energies blended, how easy it was to sit in this way with this young woman. He distinctly felt the blessings of his ancestors extending far back into the Dreamtime, where everything is reconciled from the get-go and all the way along. Aiyana wondered if they were embarking on a long journey together, and years from now they would be like Wu and Daphne continuing to strengthen their practice with each other, as familiar as one's guardian angel. They chuckled simultaneously, as if they were sharing the same thoughts.

All four of them were becoming aware that they were sitting with numerous others, all of whom seemed quite ethereal. They were one powerful thought field together. "We are here to redeem you."

"What does that mean?"

"To bring you back in alignment with the Universal Source and Intent of All Creation."

The voices came from various locations around their disk of stone:

"To redeem you from this made-up world of fears and addictions."

"That the lost be found again."

"There will be more support and power to live in the right way."

"Certainly no more wars."

"How can you make that happen?" The question formed in Wu's mind.

"We have the power to neutralize all weapons. We would prefer that humans give them up voluntarily, but we're afraid you may be far beyond that possibility."

"This is divine intervention. Still there will be the same pattern. Many will be called. In fact, everyone is being called, but few will answer."

"It's simple. Just be deeply peaceful, no matter what, even if someone decides to kill you."

"What no martial arts?" This question came from the mind of Daphne.

"If you can practice the kind of martial arts that can disarm others without hurting them."

"Your mindfulness becomes more powerful to neutralize fear, hatred and aggression. Your ability to radiate peace is the ultimate weapon."

"Many are being enlisted simultaneously to bring about this necessary evolution back to our true natures."

"Earth Mother would like to survive without being deeply scarred. She enjoys her beauty and prefers humans who will adorn her not savage her."

"We are with you from now on in a very conscious relationship, unless you reject us."

"How could we reject you?" Aiyana was unbelieving.

"You can be subjected to enormous pressure. As you know, the voices that promote the path of fear and destruction can be very loud."

"Remember to rely on each other. You all know the truth. Remind each other. This path of redemption must be uppermost in your thoughts."

"Simply always remembering to always do what's right."

"Meticulous."

"You four continue to truly love each other, and it will be easy."

"And love all your fellow humans, who mostly do mean things because of past hurts that have not been given away to any form of Higher Power for healing and soothing."

"Teach them to have compassion for themselves."

"Traumatized mammals need a lot of gentleness, a lot of holding."

"Learning to trust again. You may be the first envoy to some."

As suddenly as they had begun, the voices stopped as did all visual awareness of those who had been speaking. Everything dissolved once more into that pearlescent silver-gray oneness and peace.

All was quiet as the four slowly came out of the ethereal world full of angelic voices, unwound themselves from each other and sat again in a four-pointed circle. Wu spoke first, but only said, "Here we go again." Daphne nodded and smiled benignly.

The silence was profound and lasted who knows how long. Each of the four strongly felt their occupancy of a cardinal direction, like holding up the world in some way. Time dawdled without being calibrated. The sense of peace and safety was unfathomable, so beyond any of their usual musings. No one experienced a desire to do anything else, reposed in their recent and current immersion in the pacific unity of all existence.

A subtle shift brought awareness of the beings who had recently regaled them with wise words. They were accomplishing a slow fade-in, to be seen and felt by the four. The beings sometimes seemed totally spirit with no physical nature, capable of rowing and floating through space with ease and harmony. Then they would seem quite physical, hardly distinguishable from the four who occupied the center of the circle.

These four felt themselves changing as well, describing that same oscillation between spiritual and physical existence and all intermediate shades and combinations, as if they were indistinguishable from their angelic hosts. Arms extended to encompass the whole group. Yet there was no restriction on movement, physical or mental. Each of them knew themselves to be powerfully connected with every other member of the large group.

The group moved in a slow dance side-stepping around the circle with arms raised to the heavens, a sky turning the colors of dusk from the last glow of sunset waning into the deep blues and purples of impending nightfall. The four pilgrims felt themselves invited and nudged into the outer circle. An orange flame appeared where they had been, a radiance that appeared to spray individual beams of firelight to the heart of every participant affirming another bond among them all.

The dancing gradually became more energized and distinctly individual. The styles came from all over the world: hula, classical Indian, African; temporarily the whole group might dance one style for a few minutes with the accompaniment of music whose source was not obvious. The African drums shook the rocky earth and then were replaced with the thrum of sitar and tamboura.

The change of styles did not appreciably alter the ongoing sense of maternal love that pervaded the circle, as if all were the beloved children of the greatest, most loving mother imaginable, and her children were equally loving toward one another. The wayfarers found themselves merging into the greater circle, at times holding hands with numerous others, feeling a sense of unmistakable kinship with everyone. Wu particularly noticed the appearance of those who looked like ancient Taoists. He was one of them. Daphne saw women celebrating with regalia and offerings that looked like her circle of Goddess women. She felt their sisterhood inside herself. Coming from cultures that were still shamanistic, Atsa and Aiyana saw figures transforming into animal and plant spirits cavorting with other plant and animal spirits. For a while they were their own allies, as well as others newly discovered.

The dancing and celebration went into the night. Not quite sure when it happened, feeling more like a seamless transition, the larger circle faded away. The new members lay down around the central fire and were soon warmly asleep.

Little People

Little people with big dreams are reimagining the world.
~ Shane Claiborne

"We are the spirits who come to the people through ceremony. We only come through invitation. There haven't been a lot of invitations lately. There aren't many who still know how to move between the worlds. There are so many now who deny our existence. The old shamans are dying with no one to take their place. Many indigenous communities have no living shamans."

"So is that where we come in?" Aiyana interrupted again.

S/he chuckled. "Movement between the worlds is important. Humans have always done better when their ceremonies keep them connected with their spirit helpers."

"You and others like you, the beings we just danced with."

"That's right."

"How did we become so estranged?" Daphne asked.

"The politics of religion." S/he stopped and waited.

"I think I know what that means," Atsa said. "People used religion to have power over others. In the old ways the medicine people were always seen as servants of the people. They had power, power to heal, power to call the spirits to ceremony. They spent more time in the Spirit World than they did in this one."

"The women in Europe who were burned as witches, same

thing. They often lived on the outskirts of the village, wandering in open nature while others took care of the requirements of daily life," Daphne added.

"Take it back in time a lot farther, when most human beings were medicine people. Most people had at least some shamanic skills."

"Such as?" Aiyana was not one to leave anything unexamined.

"Shape-shifting, moving between worlds, healing or more accurately maintaining health, manifesting almost anything that was needed, teleportation— you get the idea."

It was the day after the ceremony. The cohort had returned to their base camp, a day of rest before returning to the jeep to resume their travels. S/he had indicated s/he would accompany them, at least for a while.

Wu sat in the sun enjoying the warmth penetrating into the core of his being. Aiyana came to his side and asked, "May I sit with you like Daphne does? I wanna know if Atsa and I are doing it right."

Wu looked at her steadily, then nodded, and Aiyana moved to his lap, legs wrapped around his torso. They drifted into a steadily deeper relaxation. In a few minutes Wu had virtually forgotten who was sitting with him. Her body was somewhat larger and heavier than Daphne's, which made little difference as their awareness was increasingly non-corporeal. Aiyana was an apt partner who already had a lot of experiences with non-ordinary reality. Wu was in a familiar flow, and she was right with him.

Atsa collected firewood from a side canyon. Daphne accompanied him but then fell asleep on a patch of green grass, rare in this high desert terrain.

She dreamed vividly. She was in a lush valley that was teeming with flowers and food crops. She walked among curves and rows of healthy plants, which were tended by a solitary woman. Daphne was drawn to her. The woman in the warmth of the day had slipped out of the top of her robe and gathered it around her waist. Daphne found her quite beautiful and then noticed that her resemblance could make her a sister. She was slightly taller and more buxom than Daphne with long, straight blond hair gathered at the nape of her neck. When Daphne drew near, the other woman opened her arms inviting an intimate embrace. Daphne removed and discarded her blouse with a strong desire to press into this other woman breast to breast.

Later she would reflect on such an unusual desire for physical maternal closeness. The other surprise was how much she felt she was embracing herself, while having a strong sense that this was an occurrence from thousands of years ago, and what they were doing was quite a normal and natural mode of greeting for the times. That was it, just a tidbit from the long-ago time.

They were not back on the highway for long when S/he told Atsa to slow down and prepare for a turn-off. Hardly a road, the faint tire tracks led toward the not-too-distant hills. When they reached the mouth of a canyon with a small creek flowing from it, ever more faintly, the tire tracks paralleled the creek for a while. The countryside was more verdant than the previous canyon. Bushes intruded on the narrow tracks they followed. Then the tracks abruptly ended at a small meadow. There was a scattering of wild flowers providing a rainbow splash among the greenery.

The friends disgorged from the jeep and looked to S/he for directions. S/he cast a warm smile over all of them. "You may wander," s/he told them. "Others will arrive later. This is a special place. Quite secluded as you can see."

The others looked back the way they had come and saw only bushes and other greenery, no sign of a trail, much less a road. Even the jeep blended in with the landscape. "Here we go again," thought Daphne, and a warm glow suffused her entire being.

Aiyana extended a hand to Atsa. They followed the tinkle of the creek uphill for a while before coming to a sandy ledge that overlooked an expanse of the watercourse. Aiyana sat cross-legged and drew Atsa to her. She bid him, "Sit on me the way I sat on you before."

He did as requested, curling his legs around her lower body and his arms around her neck. He felt remarkably at home and natural, which surprised him since he was in the traditional female position. He relaxed into a warm embrace. Aiyana found she loved holding him this way. She felt a different kind of power coursing through her, which she thoroughly enjoyed. The warmth of the sun augmented the warmth they felt for each other. When Aiyana noticed Atsa's weight on her becoming oppressive, she whispered in his ear, "Let's switch."

They exchanged positions and settled in. The periodic shrill cry of hawks in the distance helped them remain conscious as once again they sank into a deep state of relaxation and openness.

Without speaking a word, Wu and Daphne moved onto the land in their own versions of a Tai-Chi walk. Slow, arms extended, feet placed delicately on the earth, they casually acknowledged each other, inspiring a common flow without really trying. Their years together as wandering Taoists had fashioned them as two interactive components expressing the same balanced flow, peaceful and affectionate.

Wu sometimes reflected on the new direction his life had taken after meeting her and then being invited into the Goddess Circle, first as an honored guest and then as a full sibling of the sisterhood. Daphne felt extremely fortunate, for the second time in her life, to connect so profoundly with a teacher so solidly connected to the ancient ways, as they slow-danced far and wide across the countryside.

When all had returned to the meadow, S/he directed them to each occupy one of the cardinal points, and, when they were there, to chant in a freeform fashion using only vowel sounds.

"Close your eyes," s/he said, "and just open your mouth and your throat and let the sound emerge from deep inside your being."

Soon the sound seemed larger than what four humans could produce. It reverberated off the walls of the canyon and filled all available space in and around the meadow. It felt as if the sound itself was slowly manifesting something much more solid.

"When you're ready, slowly open your eyes," s/he suggested.

The meadow inside their circle had filled with little people. Not one of them was more than four feet tall with bluish-brown skin and long dark hair that stirred in a light breeze. The little people were indeed chanting in concert with the four friends and dancing around a central dais which was a smooth flat boulder. Most surprising was the figure who sat on this earthen throne. She was as large as the other beings were small.

Twice the size of an ordinary person and almost as broad, she was vast in every dimension and every way. Her breasts spilled almost to her belly. Her butt covered the entire boulder and gave rise to her thunder thighs, which provided pillows on which to rest her hands. She was beyond female Buddha and easily inspired the title "Great Mother" and epitomized the classic description of soft but strong. She waved her arms in concert to the chanting, sweeping blessings of all who were present. Strangest of all was the elephant who stood beside her and faded in and out seemingly in response to the vicissitudes of the chanting.

Her hair trailed almost horizontal behind her in a light breeze. The elephant was multi-colored, lots of pinks and pale golds. She periodically raised her trunk like a salute to the Great Mother Goddess. The four friends were all amazed by what they saw next and confirmed when they later compared their experiences. The Great Mother was taking long slow deep breaths. When she inhaled, dark entities and nondescript pollution rushed toward her. She inhaled it all. When she exhaled, it appeared that white light flowed from her, clarifying and illuminating the atmosphere.

Something similar was happening with the elephant. Her trunk acted like a cornucopia overflowing with all good and delightful things: delicious-looking food, fresh-cut flowers, sparkly crystalline minerals, perfectly formed women, men and animals; all the gifts of physical existence on planet Earth were endlessly flowing from her cornucopian trunk.

"One image of right relationship." These words floated in the air, perhaps emanating from S/he, perhaps from some less obvious source.

While they were watching, the Great Mother gradually laid back in a reclining position. Her body partially blended in with the earth. She lay with knees raised, legs akimbo, as if preparing for birth or sexual coupling. The dancing little people formed a coil. The lead dancer, describing everything from two-step to pirouette to hula, pranced right up the doorway to her inner mysteries. It slowly opened revealing only darker mysteries. Somehow, he became small enough and the secret passage became large enough that he slipped between the engorged folds and wrinkles into a well-lubricated birth channel. Was this little person returning to the Cosmic Womb from whence he came.

Even more amazing, like a parade, all the remaining little people unwound the coil of their compadre/comadre dance into a cosmic slip and slide, squealing on top of their group roar of emotional release. Emotions took wings and flew away into the atmosphere. Finally the elephant somehow shrunk and slid into Earth Mother's open door.

A bottomless silence ensued, a cacophony of no sound pervaded the rocks and trees and ground beneath them. Great Mother proceeded with her slow fade into her own Mother of Mothers Earth, of which she was a part, perhaps even the whole or the part that is greater than the sum of its wholes.

The four friends felt drawn to follow the little people back into their Mother's body. She grunted just loudly enough and shook her head ever so slightly, murmuring, "It's not your time yet."

Even Wu felt drawn to this powerful maternal being, understanding in that moment why the Tao is often referred to with feminine language even though it is by definition both female and male. "The Flow feels feminine," he thought. Even the flow of the robe rather than the straight stride of pants. "Our world is so dominated by the male side of things. A lot of effort is required for the feminine to gain equal voice. And I don't mean that women just get to talk as stupidly as men do. No, I want to hear the true feminine voices: the so-called witches of the Inquisition, whose magic kept their peoples in balance for millennia."

Aiyana and Atsa sat speechless holding hands and gazing into the vacant distance. Daphne wandered toward where the Great Mother had sat and lain and gathered some of her children into her loving embrace. She walked round and round that central altar and found nothing unusual. The ground looked undisturbed. There was no trace of the large rock on which she had reclined. Meticulously she traced her steps over the erstwhile ceremonial ground, finding nothing except one hole in the sand which held an oval shape despite the crumbly nature of sand.

Urged forth, Daphne was lured to explore this hole. She peered into the hole and saw nothing but receding darkness. She sniffed around the edges, which brought up pleasant memories of her female lovers. She easily could have stayed with those reveries for a while, but something drove her forward in spite of the sweet memories.

Next she inserted several fingers into the hole, which continued to hold its beautiful ovoid shape. Strangely her fingers deciphered a smooth somewhat oily surface inside what could have been a burrow. She extracted her fingers and licked. The taste was unmistakable but especially sweet and brought a flood of further memories to Daphne. Curious, she inserted her whole hand. It was easily accommodated, and soon her arm was in up to the elbow. She reached inside as far as she could. The tunnel felt more and more like mucus membrane, pleasant and exciting to touch. When she removed her arm, it was only to slip out of her robe and sandals, turn back to her Mother's doorway and slide right in feet first. The others were unaware of her departure except perhaps S/he who seemed to remain aware of everything.

Meanwhile Daphne was slip-sliding away along a seemingly never-ending birth canal. When she emerged from the slippery slide, which she had entered on the surface of Mother Earth, she was astonished to find herself in a conventional-appearing village of little people going about their regular daily activities. She was reminded of Tolkien's descriptions of Hobbit communities. Most puzzling was the light. She knew she had to be quite some distance underground, but there was an abundance of light whose source was not immediately apparent.

People greeted her as if they knew her. As a small person she was barely a foot taller than the average little person who was greeting her. She could see dwellings built into hillsides; gardens were everywhere and underground springs providing an abundance of pure water. A woman approached and asked if she would like to be shown around.

"Yes, I would, very much." After a pause she asked, "Do you know me?"

"We were on the surface with you. Your blond hair was a beacon in the darkness. Everyone remembers you."

"When you disappeared, we had no idea where you went."

"You have come to our home. Our histories tell that people from the surface have lived with us when there were cata-

clysms that made the surface unlivable. Sometimes we are referred to as the Ant People." She laughed. "Our only resemblance to ants is how tuned in we are to each other. We are
very individually creative, but we are coordinated in basic activities far beyond most human communities."

"The hive mind?"

"Yes, it is so much a part of how we live, we don't even
think about it most of the time. What is surprising to outsiders
is that most of us are also artists of one kind or another." They
had been walking, and now her guide gestured toward a collection of sculptures strategically placed in an open meadow.
Most were engagingly abstract with a certain allure. A few
were quasi-representational. There was one very large bear
half risen to her hind legs.

Daphne was amazed at the size of the community. She
knew they were underground, but they continued walking
without reaching boundaries, the walls of the cave or anything
that would have indicated their subterranean status, just endless fields and gardens and always a handful of little people
tending to the plants as if they were honored family members.
Another of the little people hailed them. "Come here. Let me
introduce you to my friends."

When they drew near, indeed, she introduced her plants
by personal names, not just their species name. Daphne was
quite charmed by how personable the plants felt. She could
almost see faces on some of them, and they greeted her with
a warmth usually reserved for long-lost friends. Finally, she
could not resist asking, "Do you know me?" She had not quite
accustomed herself to the familiarity she was being accorded.
She was somewhat shocked by the answer she received from
one of the more social plants.

"You are Daphne. We are often with you when you meditate."

Plant allies, she had never considered the possibility even

after hearing some of Wu's stories of his ever-deeper relationship with the Moonflower Spirit during their sojourn at the
village of Grandmother Xochitl. Such a broad range of wisdom
from a plant, it was not disbelief in the idea; she had simply
never considered that she might have spirit helpers from the
plant world.

"Would you like to sit with us for a while," the same plant
asked her.

"I think I would." Something about this encounter still had
her thrown a bit off kilter. She thought maybe taking the familiar refuge of meditation might make her feel more in her
comfort zone. So she sat among the lush plants. Her guide and
the other gardener chose to sit a few yards away, clearly wanting to accord Daphne her own unique experience.

As she closed her eyes and moved into meditative space,
she could feel the plants clustering more closely to her. She
felt herself surrounded by a warm protective glow. The meditation was not so different from what she usually experienced,
except that she felt more vital, as if the juice of life was flowing
in her veins, lighting up energy centers and the flow of chi.
She felt excited, an unusual feeling for meditation, which was
typically pervaded by sensations of peacefulness.

Then came the vision: she was in a cave behind a gigantic
waterfall. The waters of life fell with power and beauty, and
energized her being in a way that felt primal and fundamental
to all life. "I am the chi of all life; it flows to me and through
me, flows from me to everything that exists and then back to
me from all my children. I am the Great Mother, who has given
birth and provided nurturance to all life. I have been revered.
I have also been despised. Often those who have never known
me, who don't want to know me, also don't believe in me,
don't believe I exist. The nurturance they might receive from
me does not flow to them because of the barriers they have
erected. The warrior religions deny my very existence. I do not

support their exaltation of violence, their celebration of bloodshed. They call me devil, evil witch, one who violates the commandments of God."

Daphne felt that she was speaking these words, and yet they also came from an all-encompassing voice outside of herself, which continued, "You are my sisters, daughters and comrades. Band together and support each other in manifesting and radiating nurturance no matter how crazy and traumatic events around you may become. Sit in this plant consciousness, this ant-people consciousness so that you may have what you need to nurture those who are traumatized *in extremis*. Many will need aid and comfort, when the Earth changes come, and things, as they are, fall apart a bit. Remind the people that in the Unmanifest Realm of Oneness all is well, and all will be well again in the manifest world. When it's possible, guide the people to sanctuaries. Above all, remind the people that they are children of the Great Mother. She will care for them. She does care for them. All they have to do is ask. You know what an illusion death is. Find ways to communicate that truth."

The less universal voice of her own personality raised a question: "How do I get people to listen to me, much less believe me. There are so many apocalyptic scenarios from so many sources."

There was a long silence as Daphne returned to a deeper meditative state and waited. Then again came the voice that was both interior and exterior to her. "Encourage everyone to simply sit with their plants and listen. You will hear more the recommendations of doctors and other healers to practice some form of mindfulness meditation. Sit in your garden. Sit beneath a favorite tree. Encourage people to get their answers by listening to plants rather than people. We of the plant kingdom do not have some political agenda, some economic agenda. Our agenda is simply to thrive so that others may thrive. The most important relationships that humans have on earth is with the plants. What helps plants thrive also helps humans to thrive."

"What are those things?"

"Pure water and sunshine. When the water is poisoned and there is not enough good water for plants and animals and humans, when the sun shines too intensely because the normal filters have been disrupted, then all life suffers. The old stories are not fairy tales, meaning untrue and only entertainment for young humans. You, Daphne, learn the old stories so that you may tell them in a way that touches and influences people. Help people to understand the interconnected harmonious nature of all existence. The ancient ceremonies were designed to maintain that harmonious balance and to help humans to understand how to have a healthy sustaining role within that greater harmony. Ceremonies keep things in balance. Most importantly they remind humans not to abuse their great power by trying to take more than their fair share. It will always be short term gain for long term loss."

"What is the role of medicine or magic?"

"All humans once had magical powers, medicine power, so that they could re-establish harmony when anything in the flow of life drifted into disharmony. In the beginning there was hardly ever a need, so magic was practiced for fun and to keep up a certain skill level. Humans lived in something like a fairy realm. Humans were, in fact, like good fairies or good witches. When conflict arose, simply because people had and have the task of accommodating the mammal nature that we chose to take on as a kind of challenge, the shamans or magicians through ceremonies or simply sitting together within the greater wisdom, would help the affected humans to find their mutual harmony again."

"It sounds so easy."

"It was."

"What happened?"

"It was what drew us to animals; the raw intensity of desire and emotion was so addictive to some that they did not desire to return to the greater harmony. They thought they preferred the thrill ride of hyper-indulgence. They avoided the shamans and healers, and lost their way. They became so cut off that they could not find their way back or they even forgot that there was a better way to return to. For a long time they were confined to certain areas of the earth, while harmonious life continued in most places. They only became a problem to others when their numbers increased, and they found the need to expand their territory to make room for their enlargement of population."

"Well, we can't go back."

"True, the challenge right now is to re-incorporate enough of the Original Instructions in how to live in peace and harmony that the imbalance, the disharmony does not lead to massive destruction that would harm most humans and much of the plant and animal realms."

"It seems like it should be so simple and easy to live in harmony."

"It was and it is, except for the growth of collectives and institutions devoted only to servicing the raw desires and emotions of human beings. Colossal structures now exist, bent on pushing things more and more out of balance. It takes a lot to resist their size and their single-minded intent."

More suddenly than she arrived, Daphne felt herself beginning to leave. She turned toward her erstwhile guide, who smiled broadly, and then in the blink of an eye turned into a very large ant or at least that's what she looked like just before the entire underground scene disappeared. Daphne found herself sitting beside S/he, who spoke to her as if she'd been there for a while.

"You may have noticed that we spirit beings can assume any physical form we choose, but we find it entertaining most of the time to play by the rules of biological reality. I have taken an androgynous form to make a point, to remind you all how non-essential things like gender can be. And I enjoy playing with the characteristics of both female and male. The phenomena of emotional bonding and romantic attraction I find particularly fascinating. So unpredictable, so ephemeral, it's intriguing for a soul who knows how most things are going to turn out before they ever happen. That can get boring. Right now we don't know what the outcome is going to be."

"I just want to know what I'm supposed to do," Daphne interrupted.

"Hmm, you're a teacher, aren't you?"

"Yeah, I guess so."

"Then teach, and now you have more to teach."

"If I start talking about what I've experienced with you and what I experienced with Grandmother, people will think I'm a total kook."

"They might." Long pause and then, "You have to figure out how to teach these things to people who have little or no experience. Some indigenous people still grow up with enough ceremony, which opens the doors to the Other World, that they know the reality of Spirit as a normal part of daily life. But so much corruption has happened in the building of this palace of pleasure-seeking materialistic extravaganza. The Original Instructions, the principles of living in harmony with all life, have almost been completely obscured, to be replaced by an obsession with the power to destroy. Who has the largest army? Who has the biggest weapons?"

"What are we supposed to do? That corrupt philosophy runs the world. To resist is to be ground underfoot, expunged, liquidated."

"Over the centuries many have chosen to leave the material plane rather than try to cope with the destroyers and their ever-growing destructiveness. What we do know is we are in a time of transition. Things are different than they have been for centuries. There is potential for change. The ancient truths will again see the light of day."

"The current system will not let go easily. It is not built to relinquish power."

"The current system cannot sustain itself. Those who want to compete violently for power and control may do so to their ultimate destruction, or they may be prevented from doing so by the old souls in young bodies who will have the ability to cripple the massive weapon systems so that no one can use them. The destroyers may be saved from themselves and have the opportunity to change their ways. Every little child wants love. That little child still exists inside every human being."

"Still, it's a big leap from teaching meditation and martial arts to telling people about human ant-colony civilizations that thrive beneath the surface of the earth."

S/he laughed out loud. "I have faith in you. You'll figure out how to do it."

"Do you hug people?"

S/he laughed again. "Yes, why do you ask?"

"I could really use a hug about now."

Voices of the Other World

You are not yet in the Emerald Dream.
First, you must remove your earthly shell.
~ Richard A. Knaak

When the others returned, Daphne briefly related where she had gone. A lively discussion ensued about how many peoples around the world have traditions of little people, who are at least somewhat magical, from Leprechauns in Ireland to Menehunes in Hawaii. Daphne raised the issue of the disappearance of magic from having any legitimate role in mainstream society.

"At best it's discarded as make-believe; at worst it's condemned as evil."

"How do you know this, Aiyana?" Atsa asked.

"Western history, it's all right there. Burning so-called witches during the Inquisition is only one horrible example. As the world became more warlike, those who controlled things through violence were increasingly threatened by those who practiced medicine power or magic or shamanism or whatever it was called. The leaders of the warrior societies wanted their form of power to be superior to all others. Destroy or marginalize, for centuries any magic that survived was driven underground."

Atsa joined in her denunciation. "For centuries they had been killing the magicians in Europe, condemning them as the devil's own. So when the Europeans got here it was almost automatic to condemn us as devil worshippers, one more justification for trying to kill us all, steal our land and destroy our cultures."

"It is the primary propaganda of Western Civilization," Wu added.

Daphne turned to S/he. "So is it intended that we be part of some revival?"

"Leaders." S/he said it so softly they barely heard her.

"All of us?" Daphne exclaimed.

S/he looked at all of them and smiled, resting her eyes on each one for a moment. "You and others like you are the hope of the future."

"Clearly there's a purpose in showing us all these things," Daphne declared.

"Did you ever doubt that?"

"We have already begun," Aiyana affirmed. "The healing ceremony we did with Atsa is just one example."

"The only one I was involved in. You've told me about others."

"It seems there are more women than men who are practicing magic these days," Daphne interjected.

"Are you surprised?" s/he asked. "Women were the first because they were the first. They existed before men."

"Everything is born of woman," Atsa quoted.

"The essential truths are still there in many traditions. Often they are quoted but not fully understood."

Just then a flock of little birds fluttered into the nearby space. "Remember," s/he reminded them, "these little beings have medicine, just like the little people. It's not only eagles and owls."

Soon they were on the road again. They had not gone far

when Atsa steered the jeep onto a poorly paved side road. Within a couple of miles they came to a small collection of hogans and pre-fab houses. As he descended from the jeep, an older woman greeted him by name. Soon several children joined them, calling out his name. "Atsa, Atsa."

"This must be the blond healer you've told us about." The woman voiced her assumption.

"My reputation precedes me," Daphne thought as she returned the woman's greeting. "And I'm being referred to as a healer."

"Yes, this is Daphne. Daphne, this is Cocheta."

Cocheta turned and looked off into the distance. "Walk with me, Daphne." The woman spoke in poetry in some universal language, which was nonetheless intelligible to Daphne.

Many of the men have jobs they must travel to
Living in the Magic Queendom
*   What was it like before the contention between good and evil?*
When Magic was simply the joy of spreading joy
*   the leap of the dance*
*   the flight of the hummingbird*
*   or eagle*
*   or faerie*
Each of us has a piece of the story
*   an inkling of the glory*
*   that once was. And will be again*
A beach full of oysters and clams
*   trees teeming with fruit*
To imagine the imagination into being
*   a realm to dream into existence*
*   to fancy that and that and that*
*   and let go again and again and again*
A love erotic and chaste
*   the pure gold of purple passion*

Let us always walk together
  in the truth that we know to be the truth
Some of us in these out of the way places on earth
  have not lost the truth that we all began with

Daphne could feel the question forming, or maybe it wasn't a question so much as a thought that started as a whisper and slowly got gradually louder in her mind: **I want to know this truth.**

"No need to shout, but I do understand your enthusiasm."

As they walked, the atmosphere began to shimmer. Waves passed through the visual field. The high desert was transforming into lush fields of fruits and flowers.

Magic…medicine only has the power to soothe and coax
  like a most loving mother
Creating harmony and beauty wherever she is
  whatever children are with her
She walks in beauty coalescing
  and spreading beauty wherever she goes

"What about the people, our ancestors?"

They saw the fertility of the land our Mother Earth
  only wanted to protect her and the fruits born of her
They were the groundskeepers of the land living in Paradise
  Why do anything to mess that up?
They spoke to each other's souls
  the soul of animals the soul of plants
Understanding how it all fit together
  because they could see it
Everything discovered by science was known to them
  without needing instruments and machines in order to perceive
Lovingly interconnected interdependency of all life

"Will we live like that again?"

"You and many others must do your part. We are creating the new world right now."

"Will I be able to show others what you just showed me?"

"Not immediately but soon. Not the same vision but equal power."

"My friends and I have been shown so many things, enlisted in projects. Wu and I chose to wander because it all became too overwhelming. Couldn't decide what I was supposed to do."

"And your wandering brought you here."

"So it's all part of it, the portals between here and the Sky Realm, the journeys into deep earth."

"Yes, there are many beings still living the ancient truths. There just hasn't been a lot of room for them on earth. So they hide in the earth, in the air, in the water, even in fire."

"Fire?"

"Yes, there are people around the world in enclaves, like this one, who enter the other world through the portal of fire. The refiner's fire, one must be very pure to travel on the wings of flame."

There was a long silence. Daphne admired the lushness of her surroundings. She smelled the flowers and thought, "I wonder if it's all right to taste the fruit."

"Please do."

They looked like berries but not a variety she was familiar with. The juice burst on her palate, an explosion of joy. Without volition she moaned and then hummed. "Mmm, mmm, mmm! This would keep me contented," she declared. "No need to conquer empires or dominate anything."

Cocheta waited, allowing ample time for Daphne's delights. Then she simply said, "We'd like to teach you how to teach about us."

"Can I ask some questions?" Daphne asked.

"Please do."

"Is there a proper role for sex? I have lived as a monk. I have lived in the world and had lovers...only women."

"Does one way seem more spiritual than the other?" Cocheta asked.

"Either one can be genuinely spiritual or utterly phony."

"Whatever you're drawn to do at a particular time?"

"Situational spirituality, there can be spirituality in any situation. What do we mean? Do we mean heart?"

Much of this discussion was going on telepathically without words being spoken. Their minds were flowing in and around each other. There was a gush of squishy emotion almost like two schoolgirls who know that they are soul sisters.

"Rarely if ever is the truth an either/or proposition. Your Taoist practice teaches you this truth. Among many people the path of the monk could be temporary, for a set period of time, a stage of life. To cultivate a state of flowing love with everything that exists, and then to carry that love in the world, if you choose to live in the world, however each of us decides to live in the world."

"Wu is a monk."

"Yes."

"But we sit together, wrapped around each other. It is not sexual but it is often very pleasant and peaceful and safe."

"Partnership can be lovely. Limitations give shape to things that might otherwise be formless. There are so many possible realms, most of which are full of their own kind of beauty. So many beauty ways. Your Taoist tradition has preserved much from the ancient times. As you know, much has also been lost among the Overt Peoples."

"I have been realizing that a lot recently, but I think only because I have been shown some of the old ways. I was totally unaware of these ways, but when I saw them, I recognized them, as if from some deeply buried memory, long hidden, instantly recognized."

"We are one of the Hidden Peoples, practicing the old ways

behind a cloak of invisibility. We've also been forgotten, so even when people see us, they do not see us. We are not recognized."

"Yet you are showing yourselves to us now."

The statement hung in the air for a time until Cocheta simply replied, "It is time, and you are here. We are the ones you've been looking for. You are the ones we've been waiting for. You are our grandchildren on the threshold of adulthood."

They walked for a while in silence punctuated only by the lushness of the landscape which periodically sent a rush of energy to Daphne's heart.

"Let me show you something," Cocheta requested. She stopped and faced Daphne.

"Yes, please," Daphne responded. Her enthusiasm had been building throughout their walk.

Cocheta stood facing her. "Be my mirror," she said, as she raised her hands about shoulder high, palms toward Daphne. "Lean forward and I'll do the same." As soon as their palms touched, Daphne felt a warm glow of energy that came from the other woman but was soon suffusing her entire body, especially flowing into and out of her heart. Definitely cozy, the energy was warmly white and golden and surrounded them both in a single aura. Such an instant sensation of oneness was new to Daphne, like the long, low rumbling of love that never climaxes but rolls and flows for an apparent eternity.

Their aura continued to grow and expand until they were surrounded only by the light they had generated. As Daphne watched, the light coalesced and became a stream flowing toward some far distant goal.

"We are answering prayers," was all that Cocheta said to explain.

When they walked back, everything happened in reverse. From the lush realm they passed through a veil and were again at a very rundown-looking roadside camp. "Even this is invisible to most outsiders," Cocheta stated matter-of-factly. There

were abundant fruits and vegetables and fresh water undoubtedly brought from the other side of the veil. "Make yourself at
home," she invited. "There's more to the story." Then Cocheta
was gone.

Each of Daphne's fellow travelers had been taken on a
journey by their own special guide. Aiyana and Atsa were
greeted by someone that appeared so much a two-spirit that
s/he would appear female one minute and male the next,
sometimes a very masculine woman, sometimes an effeminate
man. As they walked, s/he talked. "You have such an opportunity in these times to be young and already you know so
much, understand so much, accept wholeheartedly what
comes to you from the Spirit World. You have grown up out
here in the openness of the high desert away from the assault
on your senses that city life inevitably creates. You have not
had to close yourself off from what's happening around you,
so you could more easily be open to the medicine power that
is all around you."

Atsa and Aiyana looked at each other. They were not often
told that their distance from civilization was a blessing. They
might have suspected at times, but now it was being blatantly
confirmed.

"You are young and in love, a couple. I have some sugges-
tions for you. It is very important for you to fulfill your destiny.
Anything that gets in the way of that is not a good thing. Can
I be very pointed in the advice I will give?"

The young couple again looked into each other's eyes. The
mutual acceptance of whatever was coming to them was already implicit in their nascent relationship. They nodded and
looked back to their guide, who continued. "Nothing is really
bad. Simply, some things are better than others. In a relationship you can become sexual, and that opens doors into pleasure, emotional bonding, adoration and even total immersion.
These are all good things. There are other less-well-known
ways of being that are only available to those who forego the

sexual path, at least temporarily. To walk the medicine path requires everything a person can bring to the ceremony. It presents a handicap to direct our energy into sexual experiences when we need that energy to work effectively with the medicine. Are you with me so far?"

Both young people nodded enthusiastically, this time without looking at each other, although there was a subtle squeeze to the hand each still held.

"You can support each other, work with each other, be medicine sisters and brothers. Sometimes that's better than sex. You will be working together. It is a grand adventure. medicine, magic, shamanism, spiritual healing, we use many terms from many ancient cultures to describe a single set of phenomena which are universal and available to those who quest for them and are chosen to receive them. All of you will learn as much as we know about the true history of human beings on Mother Earth, how things were in the beginning and then little by little became less and less ideal."

"I want to know that!" Atsa blurted.

Aiyana chuckled and added softly, "I feel the same way."

An old Indian man came for Wu, as if from another time before the troubles, before all the death and destruction. Wu thought of him as Indian, because he couldn't tell if he was from Asia or the Americas. Silently they walked together for a while. Neither had words nor a desire to speak. The old man stopped and motioned for Wu to sit with him. They sat together in the sandy soil, and the old man brought out a long-stemmed pipe. He filled it one pinch at a time with a mixture of herbs. Each pinch was held to the sky and touched to the earth before being placed in the red stone bowl. He held the pipe to the sky, touched the bowl to the earth. Once lit, the pipe was offered again to sky, earth and the circle of the four winds. They passed the pipe back and forth until there was no more smoke. Then everything went blank for a while.

The next thing Wu remembered he was walking through a lush forest with the old Indian. They came to a pure blue lake. From the lake emerged an ethereal being, shades of white and shadows. She slipped through the air as if she were air itself, but sparkles fell from her like snow in the glint of sunlight. As they stood there in awe, she entered into both of them simultaneously.

"So this is what enlightenment feels like," thought Wu, and then again there were no more thoughts, just a pool of warm white light that twinkled.

Then a voice:
Beginning and end of all things
only taken from a time beyond time
the beginning before beginning
no starter's whistle, a continuum
flowing and flown above mountains
below oceans brighter than fire,
I am all these things and so are you.

A different voice:
How did it become all about survival?
I love my children, my people
You are all my people
from the beginning of time
before the beginning of time.
Can you not be mothers to each other
as I am mother to all of you?

She was undine and sylph and much more. She took a hand of each of them. They ascended, three as one, and flew through the air together. "My mother," the old Indian appended in the voice of an affectionate child. "Let us all emulate her."

From the beginning of this journey Wu had no idea of destination. His practice had prepared him for such uncertainty, and he was reminded of his explorations with Toloache. Nature spirits, elementals, angels all seemed to be part of the ongoing story, the prophetic information that was becoming destiny for him and his young friends. So many faces of the deity, Goddess Mother in all her beautiful perambulations, he awaited the latest installment as they skimmed a cloudy atmosphere on the way to somewhere.

"Flight, sometimes called magical flight, is different from disappearing in one place and appearing in another," s/he addressed the young couple. "One of my names has to do with flight. You should have a name to call me. Please call me Zephyr. Play with it as you would a jazz riff. I like your names, Atsa and Aiyana. You sound like partners. You sound trustworthy. You sound like people I'd like to know."

The distant call of a hawk brought all their minds to attention. "Let us sit and soak up the rays of afternoon sun."

It was a castle on a great cloud of unknowing, where they came to rest after flying as one bird into this stratosphere of air and vapor. "Cloud of unknowing, a goal in some systems," thought Wu. Their guide twirled around them as an invitation to rest upon the pillowy cloud.

Daphne lay among the seeds of a gigantic cut-in-half squash. The seeds provided support and massage at the same time. The gentle golden orange flowed in her and through her in easy curves and slow-motion pirouettes. "God/dess is sensual. If our sexuality was truly guided by spirituality, maybe there would be less damage done. Compassion for all, including self."

"Right track," reverberated through the fields and trees.

"Voices that have no explanation, that require no explanation. Great Mother lying among her myriad seeds, honoring each other, a perfect image of her inside each seed. We carry the DNA of Goddess and God. Can we realize our potential?"

"It's what we're here for." A reverb vibrated in her body.

"Is every day like this?"

"Every day is differently beautiful," said a gentle voice, beside her this time. "When magic was always done without malice in the long-ago times, life was unguardedly awe-inspiring. We spent our time treating one another. The gift of giving felt even better than receiving. 'Tis more blessed to give than receive.' Those were not empty words. The blessing of giving joy to another redoubles one's own joy."

"It's a blessing."

"And just about anything is possible."

Atsa and Aiyana found each other's arms and soon were wrapped around each other like Tibetan deities. They even felt deep blue. More comfortable each time, their meditation/communion with each other had the added element of romantic attraction.

"If you can ride that wave, your medicine will be strong and brave and true."

The meditation in the arms of the other was becoming, for them, casual like a favorite place in nature that always elicits a reliably unreserved longing and satisfaction. To be there is to be mindful and ecstatic.

"To move from this place is to destroy perfection." Then the voice burst into raucous laughter.

School

Learn as if you were to live forever.
~ Mahatma Gandhi

B y conventional standards, the circle that assembled the next day would probably be judged shabby. Their clothing appeared old and dirty. These dark-haired, dark-skinned *Indios* epitomized the stereotype painted and repainted by the propaganda of the dominate-by-violence society. So-called civilization had used this stereotype to shun and marginalize and oppress indigenous people for centuries. They were shadow-beings whose image has been perpetuated by churches and governments for as long as there have been empires. The four friends stood out as cleanly different, not subjugated, but naively in possession of a core essence of themselves.

Even their guides looked shabby in the light of this new day. Zephyr spoke first. "We are projecting an image to demonstrate how much old prejudices you've been around all your life influence how you view everything. People have shadows. Be aware of them. Let them teach you." As she spoke, she faded in and out of the ragged, destitute, misbegotten image of utter poverty materially and spiritually. Slowly s/he transformed into the gentle breeze of her name and back to the filthy drudge hag.

When Aiyana laughed, it broke the tension. "That's really

good," she exclaimed. "Can I do that?" As soon as she said it, she began to morph into a decrepit old hag and then back to the beautiful young girl she was known as and beyond to an ethereal sylph of grand beauty. She and Zephyr took to the air and swirled and danced showering sparkles of light among the circle.

"So we don't have to pass through the veil or anything special. We can sit in this circle and practice magic with each other for the joy of it." Daphne didn't know she had spoken out loud until she looked up at a gathering of gentle eyes and smiling faces. At that moment she felt the love of the grandfathers from long ago, those who literally sat on clouds and contemplated and loved their children and grandchildren unto many generations.

To Wu these were the Taoist masters, who still sit hidden among the high mountains of Asia except when the rare person seeks them out or finds them by accident. He wondered out loud. "This is more than the usual few. It feels like a hand will be extended to many, and many will accept. We have seen people living ideal lives, creating no strife among themselves, fostering harmony and intimacy throughout the network of all life. Can many more learn to live this way?"

Atsa added, "I somehow came here after the healing ceremony at Grandmother's place. I was so open; it was easy to see and accept. Most importantly I was invited back. They seemed to know all of you. I think you were still in my aura from the ceremony. 'Come back; bring your friends,' they said. I am honored they want to pay attention to me. I was pretty lost before the healing ceremony. I'm a new person."

"You are your True Self," Zephyr added and blew him a kiss. Everyone saw the rosy heart pass through the air between them and into his heart chakra.

The next day the four friends gathered with members of the village. Zephyr took the lead. "It is important that you know our history as we understand it, as it has been told to us as children for longer than anyone can remember. We who live between the two worlds know this to be a true story. We know that there are many creation stories on earth. Each of them contains some truth; they've also been embellished by political considerations and the goal of manipulating people into having power over them. The Bible is an excellent example of stories subjected to the machinations of priests and rulers to produce a tightly controlled system.

"The story that you will hear today, and in the days ahead, has been held in its pristine condition in the other world. It has not been subject to the same process of variation and deterioration that happens to stories on earth. It has never been altered for political purposes. It is important that you know this story. It is the basis for living a life of peace and joy on earth. It is a template or a set of guidelines about how people lived in the right way before anything else happened, before they learned other ways. This story is deeply embedded in all our souls. It is the story that you must know as well as we know it. It will be the foundation of your teaching of others. It is the harmony underlying all magic, medicine and right livelihood. Any questions?"

Daphne asked, "Can you summarize the theme of this story?"

"It is about the origins of human life on earth and the lifeways and principles that facilitated harmonious partnership among all humans for millennia." Zephyr waited. There was no sense of urgency.

Wu asked, "So this is way before the systems that we know of now, the great religions, the myths and legends of the Greeks and others."

"Yes, however, those of you who are familiar with these earthly philosophies will see that the great teachers were attempting to communicate this ancient essence in increasingly difficult and violent circumstances: Jesus, the Prince of Peace; Lao-tzu, the Way of the Tao; White Buffalo Calf Woman, the pipe ceremony to bring peace and resolve enmity; Magdalen, whose knowledge of the old ways made her a target of patriarchal priesthoods and violent governments. You get the idea."

"Even the Catholic nuns found ways to immerse themselves in pure spirit, Teresa of Avila, Hildegard von Bingen."

"Yes, Aiyana, the women apostles of truth are so often forgotten in this male-dominated world that has devolved over the centuries."

"Am I a second-class citizen because I'm male?" Atsa worried out loud.

"Not necessarily. Everyone has been brainwashed by the lies of the violent patriarchy. All people who are aware are in a process of deprogramming themselves." Zephyr waited to make sure there were no more questions, and then continued. "You will hear this story many times. The first time you will hear it uninterrupted in its entirety, so there will be no disruption to the flow. In subsequent tellings, there will be opportunity for questions, discussion and the scrutiny of your beautiful modern minds." She chuckled and glanced to her three cohorts. They would take turns telling the story to the new recruits.

The Birth of Turtle Island

The events recounted here happened many thousands of years ago when the world was bathed in starlight.

It was one of those islands somewhere in the southern Irish Sea. The sea may have been lower in those days. It was a time when Shee was everywhere. Thus, Shee was with a young lass, also known as Shee, who rode on dolphins and skirted underneath the waves, and the water felt warm even though it would be judged cold by our standards today. Those warm currents from the South had brought her to this place. Her lineage was here long before the Celtic tribes arrived. Ladies of the Holy Isles, way back then, they plied their skills and wisdom on land and sea, truly as comfortable with dolphins as with other humans. Life was good and uncomplicated and playful. There was little need for powers because everything was at their disposal, yet they played with their powers because it was entertaining like an ongoing morphogenetic art show, as another fascinating aspect of the hive mind, intimately connected with one another the better to individuate.

So there they are, the ladies, the dolphins, seals, and luminescent fish as far as the eye can see, shining brightest at night and reflecting their colors off the white sheet of clouds. Like a sheathed sword of light these ladies swooped and gallivanted, horse women of the sea, playing at protecting what didn't need protection at that time. The sparkle of the blue-green waves was their reward, the leaves and berries of the islands their sustenance.

Yet something drew them unalterably west across the land to that larger wilder sea to test themselves in the arena of that larger mother's bombastic frisson, such a thrill to fly in the face of Her fiercest storms coming at the younger ladies like the most mind-shattering orgasm of natural force. Flying through rain that felt like swimming upstream to spawn. Yes, sometimes the ladies were men. They teased each other with their shape-shifting. It was the monkey-bars of their world way back then.

And then they went home to their gentler sea knowing one day they would go west to stay. Until then they were content (most of the time) to roam their natural gardens and play in their own private sea, not particularly aware that they might be awaiting a call.

When the day finally came, they were so profoundly drawn to the Western Ocean, there was no hesitation but to answer the Call. It had come; it was time. Away Shee flew and swam toward some center that Shee felt inside her own center. Out of the North came a blue-white wind that whipped the water and air into a froth that propelled her to the South, the steam heat of a tropical ocean where things were being born every day. Unavoidable this place of hurricanes, vortices, and warps in the fabric of existence from the minutest particle to everything that is. In slow motion, she swirled in this nuance of time and motion. Emotions as deep as the ocean herself taunted Shee. Until now her world had been her playground. She wished she could go back, but it was too late for that as well. Carried into this throbbing turbulent labyrinth of slo-mo but inescapable swirl and whirl of warm water, she had a sense of impending something, perhaps birth. Had Shee been so powerfully pulled here in order to be born?

There was one constant. The dolphins were still with her, her own special pod escorting her through everything that was strange and new. Shee was not afraid; it was more like the thrill of being right on the edge of something, a cliff from which to glide and soar. So it felt to be in these slo-mo tropical storms. What would it mean to be born of this place? And born into what? Sometimes Shee swam with the dolphins; sometimes Shee rode. They had been with her as long as she could remember, which was a long, long, very long time. Would they be with her after Shee was reborn. Shee did not remember ever being reborn before. No one back home had ever talked to her about being reborn, or what one gets reborn into, or when exactly it's supposed to happen. Shee was glad her dolphins were with her. With them Shee was ready for anything.

Shee felt herself drawn to the intimacy of her Ocean Mother's bed and there found herself immersed amid the gush of dearest feelings and smooth liquid propulsion, as if her whole existence had brought her to this raw edge of ultimate awe, to be One with her Ocean Mother again. Yet Shee moved and kept moving, swimming and gliding through this vast watery womb, Shee and her dolphins in perfect tandem. Floating yet moving ever so slowly in a direction was a gigantic sea turtle, who exuded a most ancient sense of primal and eternal oneness. Shee slowed herself down to drift in concert to this Turtle Mother. Shee felt so loved and so protected and so small, like a tiny baby or even a fetus in relation to this being whose energy felt as big as the entire ocean.

Suddenly Shee understood as she watched a strange and wonderful process happening right in front of her. The scope was unimaginably huge, yet Shee knew she was seeing it all. Her tiny eyes encompassed a vision of creation unfolding all around her. Shee was in many places at once, as if her eyes were not just her eyes but also the eyes of a multitudinous family of sea creatures. Shee was seeing through all their eyes too. How lovely; how delightful; how awesome!

A gigantic self-propelled half shell, the kind that Aphrodite was born from many centuries later, scooped sandy earth from the sea floor. It was more than that. It was full of life, blood and mucus and the flesh of tiny critters who lived in the earth of the sea. The body that was her body was now a mermaid. Shee loved the power of her grand tail fin thrusting her in graceful pirouettes and whirls and serpentine patterns, regarding Turtle Mother as Turtle Mother regarded her.

Shee also felt herself swimming with a double, and they had amazing symmetry. They would slow and rest, feeling each other's essence of spirit and blood, peerless mirrors for each other, part of an unbroken chain of sea women/Sea Goddesses extending across limitless time and space. A sisterhood and parenthood, reclaiming their far-flung foundlings, they could rediscover their enduring bond with all the beings of wisdom and love and medicine power. Shee, who already felt so blessed, was realizing how much she'd been missing up until now, that fuller connection we all crave whether we know it or not. Shee had such wise mothers and sisters back home by the Irish Sea, and now this?

"All in due time," a voice answered her back. "There are many stages in a woman's life. Everything is preparation for what's next. So far your path has brought you to this place. To be here at this time is indeed a blessing. As you can see a major birthing is happening."

Shee knew better than to look around for the source of the voice. Instead she noted how Turtle Mother, with an enormous mound of sea earth on her back, was slowly, ever so slowly, rising toward the light above. Shee marveled that, somehow, she was a part of this birthing. What Shee had anticipated as a personal birthing had become so universal, so enormous. Shee chuckled at her previous naiveté.

Shee rose ever so slowly accompanying Turtle Mother in her long leisurely ascension to the surface. One layer she passed through was inhabited by thousands of rays. The undulation of their fins was mesmerizing. Luminescent shades and hues shone through them. She could feel herself begin to take on their lithe shape and supple shimmer, and then they were gone, and Shee was in another layer of so many. Shee was glad the process was taking so long. Shee felt so at home in the depths of the ocean that she didn't want to leave. Shee also knew that eventually she must. It was an inevitable part of the journey. Shee and Turtle Island would be born together after this long journey through the saline waters of life. Shee did not have names for all the fish she saw. Their phosphorescent colors tickled her brain.

There were gigantic sea horses of gold and blue and pink. They were large enough to ride and larger. Then Shee passed through a village of jellyfish wafting and undulating to the waves inside the sea. There was the greatest commotion and sense of turmoil and yet simultaneously a pervasive aura of peace and tranquility. Shee swirled yet also floated. The giant Mother Turtle appeared to hardly move at all at the center of this multi-dimensional, multi-faceted process of birthing and creation. The earth of the sea was rising to the surface of the mighty ocean. Shee rode with Her, now riding a sea horse that looked more like a horse, a white horse with a long wavy mane and a huge heart. They rode with the speed of their passionate hearts as Turtle floated upwards ever so gently. Which time warp were they in, the slow trance or the fast dance?

This journey went on for what we might call many days or many moons. Shee became and/or rode, swam, and flew with or on many of the myriad sea creatures. There were not rigid rules about form and structure and maybe just a greater multitude of variations on the theme of life. Immense octopi floated by with the delicacy of jellyfish. Shellfish of all shapes, sizes and colors seemed suspended in space next to a similar collection of starfish, anemones and neon urchins lighting their ever-changing path.

One day or night or space in time they could see that they were nearing the surface. There was an orange glow that came and went quite regularly. It was minuscule at first but gradually grew larger and larger.

And after another space of time, Mother Turtle and Her Entourage broke the surface and entered the open air. Shee discovered the orange glow came from an orange globe that she gathered was quite some distance away. At first Shee had to dip back into the water in order to breathe. She and her dolphins and other beings could feel something growing in their chests alongside the gills that had worked so well for drawing oxygen out of water. Other sea creatures elected to remain with those who gathered their breath of life from water.

As Mother Turtle now floated on the surface of the ocean, periodically the orange globe disappeared and darkness lay upon the waters mitigated by tiny sparkles of whitish light and sometimes by a silver globe that gradually shrank into nothing and then grew again to become perfectly round. Shee could see that Mother Turtle was growing. Her shell and the sea earth on top of it were spreading out across the placid ocean, visibly expanding before their very eyes.

Shee wanted to crawl out of the water, and so she did. Her lungs were working quite well, and Shee noticed the heat of the orange globe upon her skin as soon as it dried in the warm air. Shee had almost forgotten what it was like to be on dry land in the open air in an ordinary human body, not one of the hybrids she'd experienced since she left her home on the Irish Sea. In a way Shee felt as if she had come home again, but it was a very different home.

The soil and sand were expanding along with Mother Turtle's shell. Already there were signs of new life, green tendrils poking above the earthen surface. Shee had no sense of time, how much time had elapsed. Was chronological time important? Perhaps she was in the eternal Kairos, the everlasting

zen moment, because most of the time, time did not even oc-
cur as a concept in her mind. However, creation did seem to
be moving along at quite a pace.

Some sea creatures had already transformed into singing
birds. Their serenades filled the air. So much was forming and
changing, Shee could not grasp it all. Shee began to wonder
what was in store for her. Shee decided to leave the shore and
explore the ever-expanding land. It looked and felt more and
more like land. The sense of it ever being a turtle shell was
dissipating rather quickly as Shee walked inland. Her dolphins
had become deer and moved with her. Shee wondered what
or who she might meet up with in this new land. Shee was
walking toward the setting sun with the rising sun to her back.

As Shee got more and more accustomed to walking, Shee
found a rhythm, neither slow nor fast. It was the meander of
grazing animals, and her deer set the pace. Sometimes they
ran, and Shee ran with them, not for any reason, just because
it felt good to run. As Shee continued, there were many beings
who had appeared on this land, who looked as if they belonged
to this land, as if they had been born of it. Shee did not know
them or have names for them. They were different from her
four-legged friends back home. Some were similar, and so
Shee named them accordingly. There were deer, who were
clearly deer but different and larger than her deer or any deer
Shee had ever known.

Sometimes when Shee ran with the deer, she became one
of them in order to run with them, even though in her two-
legged version Shee could be as swift as the wind. Shee was
also quite impressed with the large shaggy grazers with
curved horns. They seemed to be such wise beings, quite at
peace on their grassy plains. There were woods with tall trees
interspersed with the meadows and plains.

The brown shaggy grazers communicated with her, mind
to mind, mostly expressing feelings of peace and balance as
they wandered this pristine land. Days and nights went by in

this reverie. At night Shee curled up with her deer for restful and blissful sleep. One day they came to a low cone of land. They went toward it. From the center of the cone a magnificent being was emerging. This womanly figure with bronze skin, on hands and one knee, arose from the center of the cone. She had the face of Mother Turtle and somehow rotated so, without moving a muscle, this stunningly beautiful woman was able to survey Her entire landscape: the Four Directions and every increment in between. Then Earth Mother slowly stood and grew before Shee's wondering eyes.

Goddess of this land, Creator-Goddess combining earth, wind, fire and water to set in motion an evolution of Soul and an evolution of Form. Evolution is a kind of shape-shifting that takes place over time. Soulfully Shee wondered if she was destined to be more than a wanderer, if she had some higher purpose that would be revealed to her. Perhaps this Earth Mother had a mission for her. In the meantime, Shee stood transfixed in awe and reverence and a sense of infinite love. Earth Mother stood with legs spread to the earth and arms spread to the sky. Joy was written all over Her face and radiated from Her entire being.

Later Shee would remember a sense of timelessness. How long did Shee stand in a circle of beings, the inhabitants of Turtle Island? Shee could not say if it was minutes, hours, days or weeks. It felt limitless and when Shee moved on, she carried a multitude of feelings with her. Did Shee receive a mission? Shee did not know. Shee knew very strongly that she must keep roaming toward the land of the setting sun.

Along the way Shee met many more four-legged and winged ones. Shee recognized wolf and bear from back home though they were different as was the big cat Shee saw. All were friendly to her with the same sense of communicating mind to mind if need be. Shee saw people but always in the distance and never with a sense she should seek them out. In fact, Shee felt quite the opposite, that it was not yet time to rejoin the community of humans.

Again Shee could smell the sea and knew she must be nearing the western shore, growing excited in a way that confirmed to her that she was really a sea creature, one that could comfortably live on land, but felt more deeply at home in or near the sea. Her deer were excited too. They obviously wanted to be dolphins again at least for a while. When they reached the shore, her deer became dolphins, and Shee swam with them not far from shore. The sun was on its way to disappearing beneath the sea. They kept that golden globe to their left as they leaped and dove and swam their way up the coast. At dusk they came ashore and assumed their landed selves again, found a lush meadow and fell asleep together.

They continued on land for a while but staying near the coast. It was in the spirit of exploration and adventure. They had been so long in the ocean before the birth of Turtle Island, and Turtle Island was all new, undoubtedly brimming with a potpourri of happenings that were just waiting for the arrival of Shee and her deer/dolphin family. Even close to the coast the terrain was full of surprises. Already the watercourses had carved wrinkles in the otherwise green world. The water was at times as blue as the sky and sparkling white. Rocks and trees sculpted the landscape with ever-changing contours. The pace of change on land was ever so much slower than the ocean, and the ocean was slower than air and space where fairies and angels flew. Fire was the most mysterious for her, the speed with which it could consume all in its path, yet the forests and meadows and prairies grew back.

Again a considerable period of time elapsed. One day they came across a four-legged, who was impressively several times larger than the largest of them. It was gray and ponderous. At first Shee judged it to look quite preposterous, but then Shee noticed that the long tube from the center of its face was used to grasp objects. It was in its own way as practical as a hand. Shee wondered about the thinner white tubes quite pointed and rather dangerous looking. Then this grand sister began digging in the earth with her sharp sticks and enjoying the delicacies she uncovered. This great being felt old and wise. Shee saluted her and met with her mind to mind for a while before Shee and her group passed on.

The deer in this northern region had great racks of antlers and roamed in large herds. Her deer family ran and played with them as they migrated with the herd for many days.

The coastline had gradually curved until they were walking into the rising sun with the setting sun at their backs. Shee began to have many thoughts. Shee had been merely living in the moment and delightedly so for so long, it was novel to be thinking, analyzing, synthesizing. An odd question arose in her mind: What is my purpose? Did Shee have a mission beyond this open-ended exploration of New Creation? She was loving it but also began to wonder if it was leading somewhere. Shee knew she was seeking a new vision of her Self, beyond the girl who had left her home by the Irish Sea so long ago. Shee was growing from all the marvelous experiences, but nothing yet qualified as a vision. Yet somehow Shee knew she was getting closer.

At times great flocks of birds covered the sky and settled together in a vast system of wetlands. Shee and her deer family did not fly as birds. They simply drifted over the land and saw from above what they had seen from below. And at other times with the keen eyes of eagles and the soaring wings of angels, they could take as much or as little time to be where they wanted to be and enjoy the whole panorama in detail along the way. They had journeyed in the ways of water and earth and now took to the air with ease and abandon.

One day they landed on an island together, folded their wings, and sat in a circle together, formally joining minds. They sat this way for the rest of the day and throughout the ensuing night. It was amazing how the mind of each complemented the minds of the others. Little has come down to us about the experiences of the Angel Deer family that night. Certainly, it was visionary, and they saw and heard and felt things that stuck in their memories and influenced each of them, together and separately, from that time on. Of all the phantasmagoria of images it remains a mystery why anyone retains the ones they do and the rest fade back into the collective. The images are often symbols which unfold their meaning over lengths of time revealing a bit more just when the guidance or understanding is needed. Does each such vigil produce revelation? Time would tell.

The next day there was a lightness of being pervading the group and their immediate environment. Shee felt unequivocally that Shee had enjoyed a deeper prescience of her Self. Even though it was initially difficult to put into words, Shee knew it included a fuller sense of **belonging** powerfully to the circle of all life; **mastery**, not just of certain skills, but a mastery of that which generates awareness in her Self and of her Self; **generosity,** her own and that of all other beings contributing to a richness of flow that nurtures all, leading right into a more complete grasp of the **interdependence** of all forms of existence: human, animal, plant, mineral, spiritual, etc. For much of the night, Shee had contemplated the universal flow and the circle of all beings.

Soon thereafter they reached the farthest eastern shore of this new land, Turtle Island. Shee had a mission. Some of her family, her reflections of Self, would go with her. Others would remain behind to prepare a place for those who would come. As dove, dolphin and then again as deer their roving took them back home to the beginning of the journey. So much had happened it was hard to remember how long they had been gone. Perhaps their old friends would not remember or recognize them. How could they tell them about the journey they had been on, a journey encompassing so many adventures beyond the ken of those who'd remained at home? More importantly, how could they successfully invite their beloveds to go on such a journey themselves.

Returning Home

I t was many millennia ago that this happened, that the people of what we now call the Irish Sea went westward to a new land known as Turtle Island. These people considered themselves to be co-creators on an ongoing basis. They looked forward to meeting the people of Turtle Island, the ones Shee had seen from a distance but not contacted. Daughters of Turtle Mother, they must be magical too. The intrigue was all the greater since one of their own, Shee, had been present for the birthing of the new land and its inhabitants. Many wanted to go meet them immediately. A few were chosen to make the first journey.

"If this all works as we hope, everyone will have a turn."

This new mystery, a new land rising from the sea with a new people, such excitement in the world, all the many different creations in a process of discovering each other. So many questions arose in the minds of the people of the Irish Sea. From as far back as anyone could remember, they had known only their small group and the other beings of their milieu, the sea creatures, the four-leggeds, the winged ones, those who lived in much smaller worlds (hives or underground colonies). They knew their connection with one another. They were all shape-shifters upon occasion, so they knew how those around them understood their place in the world.

To venture in such an unprecedented way had all of them leaning into the West Wind to catch a whiff of this young land across the great water. For days they sat in council, hardly speaking, just being with one another, feeling the cliff edge of impending change, excited but already grieving the passing of the older ways and relationships within which they had found comfort and peace and safety for such a long, long time.

They did not know if they were immortals, but they had no experience of mortality. The profound source of change that had threaded its way through their lives was shape-shifting, always reversible. Were there other ways of changing that were part of this new birth? They did not know and clearly wouldn't know until they had been in the new land for a while. Perhaps the only flaw in their lives, if you can call it a flaw, was that they knew the patterns of their existence so intimately that there really weren't surprises.

The way in which Shee had been drawn into a journey with such an abundance of the new and different had all of them animated and inspired and yearning for such a journey themselves. During the council the groups coalesced, those who were called to journey immediately and those who were content to remain home for a while. Such an epic undertaking must be done in the right way. They did not want to overwhelm the new land with their presence. The initial group felt like emissaries on their way to facilitate right relationship in unfamiliar circumstances

On the day of departure they all assumed their winged selves and rose into the sky as one murmuration. As they shadowed one another's flight patterns, gradually the groups separated. One headed west with the same synchrony of motion. The other described a complex of patterns around their home while watching their comadres until they disappeared over the western horizon.

Shee and the rest of the group that flew west saw and felt such support from that part of the sisterhood that remained home. They knew themselves as fellow children of the Rainbow Light, that visited them often enough to remind them of their unity if they needed reminding. Perhaps Rainbow Light Mother was simply drawn to visit Her children once in a while. Shee was trying to remember if Shee had been visited during her journey. Perhaps there was another primary creative force behind the emergence of Turtle Island. Another daughter of Goddess gets to try her hand at creation, to be the artist that envisions and produces the work of art that hasn't existed before. The Mother Goddess of Turtle Island might not be the same one they had known for all their lives, but they were probably sisters.

When they reached the new land, they decided to keep on flying, see what they could see. Already it seemed more vast to Shee than when she had left it a short while ago. Though they flew high they could adjust their vision to see in great detail what was happening far below. The first impression among the Shape-Shifters was how much eating they saw going on and in what great amounts. They had experience of eating but so differently, a leaf plucked from a plant as they traveled, a swallow of water. The people and animals they saw on this land consumed far larger amounts and spent considerably more time devoted to eating. Shee remembered the grazers they had traveled with. It didn't seem like a lot but they were constantly eating as they migrated.

Their food was broken down and became fuel for their other activities. This was novel for the Shape-Shifters. They drew their energy directly from the air around them. Eating was a pastime at most. In unison they thought that this was a very different creation.

On another day they decided to adopt cloaks of invisibility and walk among the other humans. Their bodies were somehow more dense. They talked quite a bit. They seemed friendly and affectionate with their family or clan. They wandered together and gathered food, but it was easily procured. There were now many fruit trees that yielded delicious treats and the seeds of many plants. Life seemed easy, but there was another strange difference. There were small humans who followed the larger humans around and some who were being carried by their larger counterparts. This phenomenon was not familiar to the Shape-Shifters. They were all equally ancient, and familial with each other in a sisterly way.

When they flew back to the eastern shore and gathered in council, wonderment pervaded their circle.

"We must investigate further to understand the nature of these small beings."

"How shall we go about making contact?"

"We should look similar to them."

"Yes, we're just neighbors you haven't met before."

"They will offer us food."

"We can dematerialize it before we swallow it."

"Of course."

"So we fly in near their settlement, assume bodies like theirs and walk into camp."

"Let's not rush this. I think we should learn all we can before we make first contact. Inevitably our appearance will become the stuff of legends."

"That's right. First impressions are powerful. We want to build a good reputation."

Thus it was decided to do more reconnaissance, perhaps separate into smaller groups to more quickly expand the group's understanding of these differently organized humans.

The first shocking report came from a group who had witnessed a live birth. Nothing in their previous experience had prepared them for such an event. At least they now knew where the small humans came from. They still didn't know why things were that way.

Another group had observed the coupling of these humans. Apparently they came in two types. One was similar to

the Shape-Shifters. The other had an extra appendage between their legs that could grow and become rigid and then
be inserted into an opening that the first group had between
their legs. The humans seemed to enjoy this activity and
choose one of the opposite group to regularly engage in such
play.

"Yes, the animals do something similar."

"How strange!"

"Is this how the small humans and the small animals come
to be?"

"A beginning, perhaps."

"The joy that they feel in this activity feels like our joy in
flying or swimming or dancing."

"It creates a special bond, but we all have that bond with
each other."

"Why do they need this other activity?"

"Clearly this is an otherly creation we have come upon. We
have a lot to learn in order to understand."

So the Shape-Shifters remained hidden and contemplated
the extraordinary people who inhabited this land they called
Turtle Island, based on Shee's accounts of the initial creation.
Shee reflected on the life that she had known for such a long
time. Her call to the fertile equatorial ocean had changed much
of what she had relied upon as reality. They were all fascinated
by this alternate reality unfolding before them as they rambled
in all the directions and gathered impressions of the people,
animals, plants, and rock formations. Designs of water, designs of sand and the almost invisible lines of energy and the
clear sense of emerging ley lines they could see from above: all
of this but above all was the sense of mystification about these
new people, so like their sisterhood yet so different. Were they
able to shape-shift?

At the end of each day the group of sisters returned to
what had become their home base, the eastern most tip of the
island. It seemed that they could feel the land continue to

grow, but did not have a clue as to how that was happening. One evening one of the groups returned quite a bit later than the others. They took their place in council, which was their daily habit of communion. The late group was holding a powerful image which, of course pervaded the whole group. There were also many words in their minds.

"We saw the strangest thing happen."

"We had watched this one woman grow larger and rounder as we continued to observe her."

"As we watched the opening between her legs expanded and opened up and a small person slipped from inside her body."

"We have seen such small beings before."

"But never watched one emerge from inside the body of another."

The other women might not have believed their words but the moving images that came to them were overpowering. They knew they were seeing something very special even though they didn't yet fully understand it.

"Maybe this is how they shape-shift."

They tried, as people do, to understand the new through what had been seen and done in the past.

"The animals also have little ones."

"Do you think they shape-shift in the same way?"

"More observation."

They returned to their silent communion, trusting that eventually they would understand the nature of this strange new world and its inner workings. The light and colors were different. Back home was more the colors of the sea: blue, green, gray and filtered light. Here was full of warm colors. Even the green of grass and tree seemed to radiate a golden light. Hanging around in many minds was how to make contact with these people of Turtle Island and how they wanted to present themselves.

"Who do we think we are?"

"Believe we are..."

"We have not thought of our story for so long. We've just been living."

"It didn't seem important to have a story."

"Now this differently magical story is taking place right in front of us."

"Do we have a story to tell them?"

"What do we actually know about ourselves?"

"We know our being."

"We know how we've been living."

"So many questions."

"Why or how was Shee called to the southern ocean to be part of this birthing of new life and new land."

"Obviously we're supposed to be part of this."

"Our group saw something that looked like ceremony."

"Some of us or maybe just one of us could appear in the middle of a ceremony. That would give us a kind of legitimacy."

"I like it."

"Ceremonies are pretty similar: dancing, singing, rhythm."

"The joining of the seen and the unseen."

The minds went silent for a while. Lovely images and feelings floated through the communal mind. They felt a step closer to first contact. They felt more connected with these ones, their distant relatives.

"We could definitely do ceremony together."

"That could be our proposition."

"This is exciting!"

Shee remembered the waves of excitement that she had ridden and passed through since she first heard the call and knew she must answer. And now was the joy of sharing the journey with her sisters. They drifted into a deeper state of relaxation. They were still mystified but rather content with how things were evolving.

Thus it was decided that one of them would make contact

with one of the groups they had been observing and offer to do ceremony together. Her sisters were insistent that Shee be the one.

"You've had such a longer relationship with this whole process. That might be important."

It was agreed that everyone else could hover nearby in a cloak of invisibility, ready for whatever happened next.

Shee descended in the woods near the village they had chosen. Then she walked into a circle of people, having shape-shifted so she didn't look remarkably different from them. Her mind gradually adjusted to the verbal language they used to communicate before she allowed them to notice her.

"Where did you come from?"

"I am a visitor from the direction of the rising sun. I was sent because we would like to know you."

"So you're not alone."

"My friends are nearby."

"We would like to meet them."

"How many shall I bring to meet you?"

"How many are you? Is your whole group larger than ours?"

"No, much less than that."

"Then we'd like to meet everyone. We've met our neighbors from the opposite direction. That went well."

"Should I go now?"

"Yes, we'll await your return."

The mingling that resulted seemed perfectly easy and natural as if this was not their first meeting. At times the sisters became overwhelmed by so much verbal communication and had to tell the other people that they just weren't accustomed to talking very much.

"It's not like there's a right way or a wrong way. We're just coming from different places."

"So how do you live your days?"

"We might sit together in silence from first light until

dawn watching the colors of everything go through their changes as the sun rises out of the ocean to warm and illuminate our day."

"What do you eat over by the Eastern Sea?"

"That's something else. We seem to survive on very little compared to you. It's as if you are often deriving much enjoyment from eating."

"Yes, things taste good. Hunger is assuaged, and that's pleasant."

"You do ceremonies?"

"Yes, we do."

"Can you tell me about them?"

"Sure, they are more like celebrations."

"What do you celebrate?"

"Everything." She laughed. "Life, joy, family, everything that we have."

"Have you always been here?"

"I know no other place. I don't know how long we've been here. Some of us feel that at some point in time we came to be as we are right here, fully formed from the beginning. Then we have youngsters who were born here and are growing up here. I think we're all kinda new at all this; whenever there's some challenge we have to deal with or figure out, at least one of us has the knowledge we need."

"Yes, we experience something similar. The wisdom of the universe is available if we need it."

"So you have everything you need, as well."

"Yes, we do. It's quite marvelous this creation thing that we're involved in: you, me, our peoples, the other peoples on Turtle Island. We're variations on a theme that goes back to Goddess."

"Yes, we're quite certain She gave birth to us and is always ready to help us when we need Her."

"What a blessing!"

As they were leaving, they received an invitation.

"You're welcome to stay, if not tonight, then some other day when you're more prepared."

"Yes, definitely another time."

When they were halfway to the woods, they turned and the bronze bodies of the entire community, backlit by the sun to create such a rich, earthy hue, left no doubt that these were people born of the earth.

The Shape-Shifters had not socialized outside their own sisterhood for as long as anyone could remember. They had to acknowledge that the people of Turtle Island were better at it than they were. As they spent more time with their new neighbors, they were also impressed with how everything seemed to flow so easily in a life that seemed more complicated than their own. The villagers actively encouraged certain plants to expand their territory. They had knowledge of so many species and their value to the well-being of humans. This earth-based knowledge and the sheer number of different plants had not been a part of the Shape-Shifters' realm. These were earth people connected to the land in an organic way.

Their ceremonies were also focused on the fertility of plants and the life-force that was seen as all pervasive and fundamental to the continuation of their well-being. It turned out that the coupling the Shape-Shifters had seen was not a common occurrence and when done was an outgrowth of an intensity of love connection between two people and the desire to produce a small human being. Both groups derived most of their day-to-day pleasure from various forms of communion which included dancing, singing, sitting silently together and games that were mostly oriented toward entertaining the small people although everyone joined in.

Even with all the extra factors, existence flowed seamlessly, a perfect harmony, perhaps more accurately, a true work of art, this earthly creation. They did not shape-shift as the sisterhood did. Their shape-shifting involved the gradual deterioration of physical bodies, that no one was particularly alarmed by. They would cast off one physical shape and be re-born into another one after a brief or lengthy sojourn in a world of pure spirit, pure light, the cold fire of rejuvenation that warms our bodies back into life.

In the Beginning...

*A people without the knowledge
of their past history, origin and culture
is like a tree without roots.*
~ Marcus Garvey

"Indeed there was an understanding among the people that the dissolving of biological forms in what has come to be called death is simply another veil that we pass through in our existences. Distances great or small, macro or micro, universes within universes. How did so many on earth forget the few simple truths we had in the beginning: everything is permanent and ever-changing and therefore ephemeral. You are just beginning to know the multiple dimensions you are capable of existing in."

How did this happen? Daphne wondered.

"You came into this enclave where ceremonies and other practices keep the door open. We tell these stories to remember how pristine and full of promise we have been here on earth."

"Will you be telling more stories?" Aiyana asked.

"We'll see what comes through...us all." S/he swept her arms in a great circle, trailing streamers.

"Can I learn to do that?" Atsa asked.

"Probably." S/he winked at him and immediately morphed into a female Buddha with deep blue skin contemplating everyone in the circle equally.

Wu sat facing her feeling that they were conjoined even though they were several feet apart. An ornate design of diamonds surrounded them in the air of their broad auras. Wu was transfixed by the power of her contemplation. At the same time, s/he was a loving Mother, totally safe.

He could have crawled on her lap like a small child, but didn't.

The circle was also illuminated by a ring of blue-white light, quite electrifying and soothing at the same time. For the moment everyone sat in meditation somewhat generating/allowing the flow of energy that was producing the light in concert with other unseen ones. Such were the meditative interludes that were interspersed with the storytelling.

"She has always been known as Changing Woman, for She is everything that ever has been, is or will be. She is all of us, and is happy when we are happy. She is ancient, older than all the tribes, older than the moon and stars, for She is also the moon and stars. I know her because I dance her. She lets me totally be her for an ecstatic while. I fly through the air with the greatest of ease with so much joy. All you have to do is pay attention. She is there!"

A collective vision rose out of the land of this high desert. She was huge, all outlined in white, not scary at all, rather inviting. She motioned for everyone to gather at her feet and place their hands on her white light moccasins. As the small group joined through touch, a very safe yet exciting feeling came over the community. Each person was on a journey back through time, through all the incarnations, back to the time of pure Spirit, back to the oneness in the arms and womb and aura and sustaining rush of love of being in a total state of Oneness with Her; and then all the way forward again through the years and generations and beautiful beings of every shape and size and color of human.

Aiyana fell in love with an indigo boy with dark pools for eyes, and then in another instant he was gone. So many impressions and so much beauty for such a long, long time. So many millennia.

Wu was in a cloud garden full of flowering trees and a female Immortal. She beckoned to him. He floated close enough that she reached out, placed one hand on top of his head and the other over his heart; and then she was gone.

Daphne found herself in snow but she was warm and covered in tan fur like a cougar. Another cougar was licking her neck, and she felt really warm inside.

Atsa was in a thick steamy jungle. His familiar was a python; he felt its enormous strength. Wrapped around another animal, crushing, eating, transforming. No loss. Tides remodeling sand. The strength remained.

"There will be many journeys as we explore from this side what life was like in the long-ago times." S/he projected this thought into all their minds.

"So detachment was taught from an early age?"

"It wasn't so much taught as implicitly known from birth and never forgotten. So much that became encoded in the religions of earth was simply known and understood in the same way as electricity is taken for granted in modern times."

Wu felt the ring of truth reverberating in his body and mind. "So all the training that we do to be mindful and openly aware, it was child's play in the beginning."

"Yes, it was the foundation upon which humans lived and breathed, in the same way that we take for granted that children will walk and talk, the acquisition of this universal understanding was a normal everyday occurrence."

"It sounds like the children were all little Buddhas." Daphne entered the conversation.

"Yes, they were, but they also had the ability that we so love about children; they could let go of everything and just play. To be totally present in moments and interludes of joy."

"The spontaneity of children, we just love to play with them," Aiyana added, as if it had been a long time since she was such a child.

Zephyr laughed freely and easily. "Yes, even in these modern times, they still have that connection with the other world, until the world of machines and electronics grabs their attention with increasing frequency, demands a different kind of narrowly focused attention."

"Kids say the darnedest things." Wu quoted a TV show from his brief interlude of normal average childhood, which brought another laugh from Zephyr.

"What is called imagination is really vision. They are still talking with the angels. That's us and others like us. We are called by many names, but still recognized by some as very real. It's just hard when life is full of streets and buildings and machines to be maintained. There's not a lot of room for us. The entire field of consciousness is mostly filled up."

"So," Atsa exclaimed, "your enclaves are out in the country, like this one, where you have space to create in the ancient ways."

"Our presence is a manifestation of what used to be, wherever people lived on earth."

"Will life on earth be like that again," Aiyana asked.

"A new golden age? Yes, with some embellishments. That's why you are here, to be co-creators. You will have time to adjust your consciousness. Your default program will be what you have learned and practiced here. Even when you go back to that other environment, you will not be dragged back into that other way of thinking and being. The path of Buddhahood is the path of the Ancients, including right views, right action and right mindfulness. The great ones have been unshakeable in their medicine power, the vision that easily generates what is called magic. We were with Jesus during his forty days and nights in the desert. His path was very challenging. Everything was so militarized."

"And Magdalen?" Daphne asked. "My friends in the Goddess Circle often spoke of her."

"Yes, we worked with her and through her. She was a direct descendant of Shee and the magic women of the Celtic Isles."

Wu wrote a poem, inspired by the discussion of child Buddhas from the long ago when earth was created and inhabited by the first spirits to take on physical bodies. He recited it when the group next gathered.

beyond choice

we were all Buddhas
   it was easier that way
   job-sharing so to speak
compassion that pervaded everything
   in the land of the immortals
it was common knowledge that death does not last
   one revives to be present with one's special ones
death is a journey one returns from
   resurrected or reborn it does not matter
like going away to graduate school to pick up a few new tricks
   then come home to take over the family business
a cooperative called Right Livelihood
   the bliss of water and fire
   magical beings propelled through space
   by their own thoughts
acutely aware that it's all an act that's chosen
   no matter how spontaneously sincere it feels

we choose one way or another
  and live with choices made
  wittingly or unwittingly
Is that a half-smile on each Buddha's face?

"We are elders. You are youngers. Elders simply because we travel between dimensions, know more than one world and are here for you so that you may become elders. You are close to that threshold, or you wouldn't be here. Atsa, Aiyana, in particular, it is heartening that once again we have humans maturing as they should when they are young, becoming wise without necessarily becoming aged. What you are doing here now with us, you will be doing on your own and teaching others. Daphne and Wu, you are already teachers, wandering the roads of America like ancient mendicants, whose offering was their teaching."

"Daphne, you've overcome the abuse of your childhood. On the healer path, the first healing is of oneself, and you are as much ballerina as martial artist. You love differently."

"How do you mean?"

"You don't fall. Many humans fall. Your heart expands without falling. You are part of a family in California, but you chose the open road with Wu, the Taoist monk, always moving toward the greater truths."

Daphne said nothing but smiled at Zephyr. Zephyr slowly shifted her gaze to Wu, who sat impassively tuning into everything around him. "It is a pleasure to know you, Wu. The earnestness with which you have stayed on your path; we love the simple beauty of Taoism, such a perfect preparation for what comes next."

Wu bowed, one hand enclosing the other, that power always be guided by wisdom, and uttered one word softly in Chinese, "*Hau.*"

A radiance slowly grew around one member of the circle. S/he was lit up by a light that gleamed from somewhere far away and from somewhere deep inside. Manifesting as a male with long reddish blond hair and a somewhat darker beard and a robe that had just transformed from plain to shiny and luminescent, he spoke as follows:

> *The people who became Earth People, they were magic people. They had lived in a world composed of magic, fueled by magic; it was ordinary daily life. Then they imagined this biological reality, warm-blooded animals, biological beings whose magic, whose ordinary reality had a different set of rules and some attractive pleasures such as food, drink and sex. They still had their magical powers from their home world.*
>
> *There was often the dilemma, to use or not use one's power to alter the contingencies of biological survival. They had chosen to live within the parameters of this carbon-based world. How much was it appropriate to alter those parameters? The temptation was always there to paint a new canvas, plant a whole new field or create new species. How much did they want to be the Gods of this new world or, instead, simply be humans engrossed in the drama as characters, not directors.*
>
> *It turned out to be dangerous to entirely forego magic. Biological reality could be mean and dangerous and violent just as often as there was spectacular beauty and joy and fulfillment. A certain level of magical meddling seemed to be an important ingredient in achieving the fulfillment they were looking for. Sometimes the magic got*

conscripted and codified as a kind of prescription for success, hardly the dancing spontaneity that characterized the enchanted atmosphere of their home world. There was often a sense of something missing, a gnawing hunger that could impel desperate measures to achieve made-up goals.

Forgetting their magical origins had been foretold. To forget why they had created life on earth was a surprise as were the increasingly wild and inaccurate versions of how life on earth came to be. Redemption might simply be remembering the true story. We came here to experience some things that required flesh and blood bodies. When origins were forgotten, the primitive make-up of flesh and blood bodies could dictate actions without vision, destructive to the original intent of creating earth, the pursuit of sacred pleasure.

"In this world, sometimes we are known as two-spirit."

"You're saying in the beginning that everyone was two-spirit and still are today but that knowledge and those feelings are suppressed, seen as weird."

"Or queer."

"Hmm, queer is normal. Queer is our birthright. Most of my female friends are gay or bi."

"Or trans?"

"That's the younger kids," Daphne insisted to Zephyr. "Gay was as far as we could go. More difficult for the guys to acknowledge their other half. But it's there, the other spirit, the yin to the yang."

Zephyr spoke of Shee, the Shee of Turtle Island. "Shee spoke to me of the principles of non-interference, which were established in the very beginning to guarantee the integrity of the experiment. The spirit beings who agreed to take part were intrigued with the question of how much external spiritual input would be required to keep biological beings on a path of harmony, peace and love.

"Shee told me, 'It was vital right from the beginning not to meddle too much in the affairs of the people of Turtle Island, but of course we flew over and observed and sometimes walked among them. We let them know we were always available to them if they really needed our help. The people of Turtle Island are spirits just like us, who chose to live within a certain set of limitations, for the experience of it, like climbing a mountain. So there were even limits on how much we could help. In the beginning their memories of where they had come from were largely intact. It was millennia later that forgetting had become the largest problem on earth, and emissaries were sent to try to remind people of their origins.'"

"Wasn't there a safe word?" Aiyana's question elicited laughter.

"Oh, many of them; they're all effective for a limited amount of time: mantras, the names of the Goddesses and Gods, incantations in special languages, prayer of all kinds."

"It must have worked better when we were all born Buddhas."

"Those are choices too. To reconcile the two spirits or put them in adversity with each other and get off on the battle."

"There's gotten to be an awful lot of that."

"We need to resume the story where we left off. Maybe if we're able to tell the whole story, we'll better understand how Turtle Island has gotten to be how it is and what comes next."

"Do we have time for all that?"

"Ever hear of downloading?"

Other members of the circle, most of whom did not even have names to the four friends, began to collectively share their understanding of the origin of what we know as human life on earth and how things unfolded over the millennia of earth-based human life. It was difficult to distinguish individuals because they did so much shape-shifting just for fun.

"For a while, hippies were able to tune into those ancient, more pristine times, feel how it felt to be little Buddhas and free children and create a temporary society which was a re-creation of that long ago golden age when all was harmony."

"The golden age is present in everyone's DNA. As the centuries ensued it became progressively harder to access that way of being, like trying to remember your own early childhood. Some techniques always remained for having some contact with how it was in the beginning. Over time the influence of the mammalian brain and the reptilian brain pushed human existence toward more conflict, more competition, more thinking in an us-vs-them context. Crises of force were met with demonstrations of force. The voices of the elders, whose wisdom might bring the society back into harmony, those voices were not always listened to."

"A warrior mentality emerged generated by those parts of the brain that are shared with mammals and reptiles. Even the animals became more violent. Thus there was more justification to live in a consciousness of attack and defense. Safety was no longer a given of human life. It was increasingly dependent on the militancy and warrior skills of what became a specialized class responsible for the protection of the community against hostile forces."

"Each incident of violent confrontation became further proof of the need to defend the community with weapons. The millennia, when humans lived in open villages and no one was considered a threat, all were still sincerely seen as family; those days faded into an increasingly misty past, which was mythologized and made to sound like it was just made of stories about the higher aspirations of humans, but these stories had no basis in fact. For centuries there was tension between those still moving in the old ways of magic and those who believed the most important power came from better weapons and the skill with which to use them."

"The magicians were tolerated as a necessary evil and enlisted in many communities to augment the militant efforts of the warrior class. If the magicians resisted being used in such a way, they might be seen as a threat. Exiled to the edge of the village or driven to form isolated communities of their own, they were no longer integrated as important and honored members of the community. Even their ability to heal might be seen as suspect and dangerous."

"Rather than accessing the beautiful life of their ancestors as guidance for living their own lives, human groups regressed into formulations hardly more sophisticated than wolf packs or baboon troops."

"Magic was used as part of the battle. The pleasure of home and family and intimate relationship was replaced by the thrill of victory and the power to dominate or kill those who competed for dominance. Even religions preached the dominion of the faithful over those who did not believe nor adhere to the new way that had unfolded over centuries."

"Magic, itself, became corrupted by all the emphasis on power and less attention to collaboration and cooperation. What had come naturally to humans was increasingly difficult to achieve and seen by the warrior class as naiveté or the realm of childish fantasy and wish fulfillment. Even when a great teacher, one of us, declared, 'Except ye turn, and become as little children, ye shall in no wise enter into the kingdom of heaven,' he and others like him were able to influence individuals, but whole societies were already too caught up in the contingencies of power and dominance games."

"Those, who remembered the ancient truths and wanted

to live them, were marginalized to remote areas of earth. In many cases, those who still knew how to walk into a fire and enter the Spirit World did so to avoid getting caught in the bloody compelling life-way of kill or be killed. We often sent emissaries when there seemed to be an opportunity to turn things more in a direction of peace. The peace engendered by White Buffalo Calf Woman, bringing the sacred pipe to the tribes of the buffalo plains, lasted for centuries until a more powerful invader subjugated those ten tribes and all their neighbors. In the modern world it was all about superior numbers and superior weaponry."

"The last seven thousand years have shown a steady increase of violent confrontation among peoples and a loss of those ceremonies and other mechanisms which might help humans maintain harmony and peace. We all come from a common source. We should be able to work together with the precision of a concert orchestra. Instead, the world is consumed with the clash of heavy metal and a form of competition, which could be harmless and fun, but instead becomes deadly. When they are told, the stories of the golden age are dismissed as 'fairy tales' meaning not true, meaning entertainment for children but having no bearing on how adults are to live their lives."

"It is time to turn this around. We must have the power to resist and survive whatever may be thrown at us. Those who would kill in defense of their narrow beliefs, cannot be allowed to win."

"To be invisible is a very useful tool. When the blow lands, we are not there. You will learn this and other skills, so you may go in the world and teach. It is possible, and there will be a new golden age."

That night the four friends were all in the same dream. With input from Aiyana, Daphne summarized the dream in a poem:

ANOTHER BUTTERFLY

Visitation

Gathering stars or casting them into the universe
fire spirit outlined in light
or we wouldn't know she was there
Floating through a galaxy of flowering fruit trees
Her own center is a lotus blossom
whose earthly beauty reaches out into space
Goddess making love to Goddess or wanting to
or simply basking in the wanton thrill of that desire
Earth mixing with fire mixing with water and pure light
and the rarefied air of phantoms and will-o'-the-wisps
Spirits that pass through us and merge with us
overlap between green leaves and blue lightning

She consorts with thunder-beings but only on Her terms
they are Her devoted children shattering rainbows
and birthing them again
wanting merely to rest in Her lap of luxury
among those lotus flowers and dung beetles of the rising sun
Every priestess and ragged fairy on a broom
thrives on the mind-blowing venom She purveys
in those days when the right dose of snake oil was a welcome
elixir
like the milk of cows or honey of bees
(choose your poison)
Is it so hard to envision a naked enchantress riding Her own feathers
a Pythoness or Pythia who recites our fortunes
while we laze in warm baths and loudly sing Her praises
Just to drift in Her aura
drift as She drifts
a tourist in Her own creation

Dance of Life

Come Fairies, take me out of this dull world,
for I would ride with you upon the wind and dance
upon the mountains like a flame!
~ William Butler Yeats

A member of the circle, who had hardly spoken before, picked up the story of Turtle Island, also obviously referencing the group dream that the four friends had recently reported.

After Daphne and Aiyana's poem, Atsa had told the group, "It was so strange to be fire, not something that was being burned by fire; to be inside the fire, part of it, bringing in that crucial fourth element, the one that feels so different from the rest. As fire beings forming a ring of fire, we felt more primitive, more elemental than earth, water and air, all of which had a certain substance to them. Fire was the least substantial, the most prone to instantaneous change and thus the most powerfully transformative of all the elements. To be a fire being, felt like unlimited potential."

The storyteller lit up like a softly glowing fire, as she began to speak:

A group of us felt ourselves moving through time and space together. When we became aware of our surroundings it was clear that we were somewhere on Turtle Island and had become the

Shape-Shifters, our ancient sisters from the Irish Sea who moved so easily between water, earth and air. We felt our lightness, the wings that could become fins, fertile earth or red sandstone.

The sisters had assembled larger and larger groups on Turtle Island. Their contacts with the people of this place had been pleasant and peaceful. The Turtle Island people focused a lot on their relationship with fertile earth. They were people of the flora in relationship with fertile earth; they combined the bioplasm of earth with the water she held for them and the enlivening light of sun to produce the immense green world and its highlights of fruits and flowers.

I had become Shee. I recognized a friend from modern times among the people of a village. She sat peacefully with her baby, as villagers passed to and fro on their way to one plant-based activity or another. Each one stopped to spend some time with baby and mother, soaking up the pure spirit that newborns exude for the first several months of life.

The Shape-Shifters and the Earth People were preparing to dance with Goddess. This joint ceremony was the largest gathering of each month; illumined by the full moon, the two peoples danced as one in communion with and honoring their living Goddess, who appeared each month and danced with them. As the groups had become more familiar with each other, the Shape-Shifters revealed more of themselves. Their wings were quite a curiosity to the Earth People and enabled them to dance in the air, swoop and soar and add to the joy and celebration of life.

But before that, Shee felt she had to make contact with her friend. When she approached her there was a mutual recognition, and her friend motioned for Shee to sit beside her. At first they simply communed and reflected.

"How strange to be here as we are."

"I like my wings."

"They're beautiful. Can I have some too?"

They giggled and Shee rejoined, "You look even more beautiful than when I last saw you."

"I think the climate agrees with me."

"You're radiant."

"I feel radiant."

"What do you gather of life here?"

"The peace and joy that are our birthright and have encompassed most of human history."

"A world that has never known war."

"Yes, hard to imagine, yet here we are, and it feels almost ordinary."

"I know. This is normal. The world we've been living in…"

"A bizarre aberration."

"Are you coming to the ceremony?"

"Yes, it's important that my baby be there. Babies are highly honored in this society. They are so closely connected with the world of pure spirit."

As the day wore on, people began to walk toward the place of ceremony. The Shape-Shifters had dispersed among the villagers, renewing connections with those who had become friends during previous visits.

Before the ceremony I had to try out my wings, soaring high above the village and its environs. Endless thunder of midnight blue, cobalt, indigo nights lit by endless stars. Seemingly limitless space to expand into, and here I was with old compatriots and comadres and some new ones, this vast sisterhood with its recent invention, men, an idea we had only toyed with before.

Turtle Island, yes, I remember this from the before time, playing that particular edge of physical earth-based reality. We had not done that before. Turtle Island was the first appearance of bisexuality, two sexes intermingling in new and quite compelling ways. Previously there was just the infinite dance, particles of light spiraling through deep space.

Earth, Turtle Island, one of many experiments in the art and science and spirit of life. In some ways Earth has gone badly, destruction of the habitat. There was such potential had the Earth People been able to stay in balance with the other elements. That's Life Out of Balance, one element dominating or one element being shunned from the circle. Everyone suffers: the Air People, the Water People, the Fire People, but the Earth People suffer the most of all. It is why we keep intervening, reminding them of the potential that was here with the birth of Turtle Island.

Life in Balance, what is that? Have we forgotten? There are Earth People who are stuck in the Earth. There is no water for their souls, nor air to inspire to go into the light of the fire because there is nothing impure left to burn, one with the light of the fire. Harmony among all beings, to hold the image of transformation even when acted out in the physical realm. It's a delicate balance, maybe too delicate, too much of a tightrope walk.

Only because the practices, the ceremonies, the meditations were not done. In the Garden all species grew in harmony. Humans could encourage, but there was always dialogue with the other being, the Deva of the plant or animal or rock. Actions were taken in concert with respect for the beingness of the other. Violence was simply not necessary in such a world. What was the temptation?

It was always supposed to be a partnership between Nature and Spirit. Some humans became enamored and awestruck by the power of certain forces of nature. At first it was child's play, mixing air and water to create a storm, fire and earth to form lava. It was the children's art studio, the children of the earth, the spirit beings who had chosen to descend into this particular experiment, and what a playground Earth was in the beginning, here on Turtle Island.

The lion did lie down with the lamb because even sustenance had not become so earth-based, so reliant on eating. At first, our spirits simply wandered the earth, human spirits, animal spirits. Plants didn't wander so much. The eating of others also began as an experiment. People were inventing things, like taste, the sense of taste and smell, the nuances and details of sensory experience, so entrancing, so likely to carry us away if we don't have an anchor in something more stable, more balanced. If we are simply awash in sensory experience, as creative children, our experiments can make messes. They might even become failed experiments or experiments with a negative outcome.

Thus, the need for a Day of Purification before too many more things happen that are destructive of life itself. Or maybe it's simply a completed experiment. It was a good experiment because even the creators didn't know the outcome, only possibilities and probabilities, and we all get to move on to something better.

"So it's all just creative play that has gone a bit awry?" Aiyana asked.

Yes, death was another experiment that took on a life of its own, a power that occupied more and more of the collective mind. Clearly there was a fascination with the profound transformation of death, especially a death that became more and more unknown, hidden and therefore mysterious. Fascination with the sensory potpourri: tastes and textures, so many things that create pleasure, what a carnival of delights, at first, a birthright, and then an elusive goal.

I am one of those air beings who got lost in earthly delights and dark side intrigue, and I found my way out again. Now I laugh at how intensely I believed some of those things and how destructive it all became, how lost the family of beings became from each other, fellow humans but also the animals, fairies, little people. How do any of us know which thrill will be the one-too-many? Join hands, meditate and visualize that portal of light. It's a gift, a quantum leap for each of us, a dispensation to shed the poison that's holding us back.

Part of it is like 'take two'. We'll start it again from the Garden with fuller knowledge of what happens if we are forgetful enough of our spiritual guidance, forgetting to look, forgetting to call for, ask for, seek. It will probably work for a very long time, and when it deteriorates, it will do so in a very different way. It's simply where we are in the cycle, but it most definitely is an opportunity.

We proceeded to the gathering that would become ceremony. The light was bright and luscious and the color of ripe fruits. It had been sometime since Shee had come to this central place, not since her first quest across the island in the very beginning. Everything was sharper, more vivid, yet soft and luxurious all at the same time or alternating in a funky spacey rhythm that lilted over the landscape. It could go from stained glass to velvet to a mixture of artists well known and unknown.

As Shee, I felt so loved, so welcomed back into this community of tribes that shared so that each person got to be in the presence of the holy candle effervescing from the very center of Turtle Island. Ice blue, sky blue, aqua blue in successive ongoing waves of liquid light seeming to be emanating from the ocean far, far below. At times this Goddess, Sister Ocean, Daughter Ocean, rode on a delicate shell, like bamboo star paper floating on this fountain of liquid light. She sat in perfect meditation clad in a gossamer silken gown and a conical bamboo hat and a sly smile of sheer delight.

The Earth People seemed anything but earth-bound. Limitations dissolved in the presence of this pure spirit. Beings of all tribes floated in a space sparkling with large diamonds of amber light. Tomorrow they would be home in their fields and forests. Today they were one with everyone and everything, elements of wind and wave as they wove ornate patterns in the air. "Yes, we're being reminded of where we've come from, so that we won't forget and get too totally caught up in the experiment of being

Earth People."

We found ourselves together in a loose drifty circle that spiraled around the fountain of light. We felt a blessing coming from Sister Ocean, pure and ethereal and extremely intimate and sensuous at the same time, as if she was personally embracing everyone who had come to be with her. No one was disappointed. Connections were felt in all directions, a gigantic matrix of audacious warmth and affection. Yet, it also felt so casual and familiar.

It was at this point that the four friends found themselves instantaneously transported into the scene that Shee had been describing. They were about to participate in a ceremony with the shape-shifting sisterhood and the people of Turtle Island. A balmy consciousness pervaded the area.

"This is what our ceremonies have been reaching for," Aiyana declared.

"Yeah, to be this comfortable in our bodies and be awesomely spiritual at the same time," Daphne replied.

Their thoughts and feelings circulated among their small clan and then rippled through the entire group. It seemed that wisdom translated telepathically. Other impressions came and went. Everything seemed as easy as sliding over a mucous membrane or licking a path across a jar of honey. They were free to float among the tribes almost magnetically being drawn back to the shape-shifting sisters time and again.

After some time, Sister Ocean removed her hat and each person present could float into her immediate presence. With each individual, she exchanged a brief kiss on the lips, and each person felt a wave of such intense pleasure pass through their entire beings. It was true ecstatic communion and the flocks of winged beings floated away ensconced inside their own private heavens, while still in the vapor of all the ecstasy surrounding them.

"All of you came from me. All of you are part of me, in the

same way that I am part of something larger, and all of us are one with the One."

After that short message, again there was silence punctuated by the tremors of each beatific kiss. Occasionally one of the fairies among them—they were all fairies or could be—rested on a tree branch and radiated a kind of beauty that made people fall on their knees and worship. She, occasionally he, was in that moment pure Goddess in all her radiant glory. Then she'd float away again and eventually another would take her place as a momentary object of abject adoration.

Everyone got to worship and be worshiped, not sure if one felt better than the other. It was about the flow and the synchrony like when the flock rose and took flight as one. To feel so connected, so interconnected, that allowed such total coordination, made it ordinary. The colors of a ripe sky were accented by formations of light and cloud and shadow that formed, fragmented and formed again. Transparent humans floated like jellyfish. They casually flowed into each other, wrapped up so you couldn't tell where one ended and the other began. Then just as casually they halfway dissolved and undulated away again.

Wu observed, "Jellyfish are the perfect meditators, rippling in tandem to currents of water and air."

Above the blue fountain of Goddess, they could vaguely see a tunnel opening up in the sky. As many gazed at the emerging tunnel, it became clearer in its lines and dimensions with an ethereal transparent quality as if composed by moonlight in a night sky. Winged beings swooped from the near end. Their faces comprised every human on earth. Their silken wings unfolded and spread, and they formed an expansive circle of radiant light above the vast group of ceremonialists, radiating at least one strand of enlightenment to every being circling within their own spiral dance, intricate interplay of gesture and pattern.

As the long tunnel emptied of angels and sylphs, some of

the earth group began to drift toward the opening. Was it rippling patterns of liquid light or mucosa beckoning them to another kind of birth on the other side of this worm hole conducted via rainbows of tropical current and slick soft honey-dripping flesh? Mysteries of interaction between flesh and light, would they be revealed, or would the journey of sensual ethereal delights simply continue, an ongoing excursion of pristine creation?

Often the drifting flight followed the kiss with Goddess. Some went directly to the portal. Others strode away as energized as speed skaters. A smaller group became very still and floated like cocoons suspended casually and carried along on the currents of space in deep meditations of pure heart, just focused for a while on the profound sense of connection among all those present, a continuum from ethereal to earthly. The kiss of Goddess, each person felt supremely special, loved like no other, loved for who she really is. That love immediately turned over and radiated to all the other beings in attendance. The minions of Goddess were all love children, capable of being loved as uniquely beautiful, capable of loving everyone else as uniquely beautiful.

It was dawning upon the four friends that they were participating in an open passageway, a worm hole, a birth canal that went in both directions with ease. This was normal and natural at some time in the distant past. Revelations and representations of this higher awareness filtered through their minds.

Daphne expressed her understanding for the group. "Earth is supposed to be one of many playgrounds for the children of Goddess, the sisters of Sister Ocean, a place to be and dance the dance of life, an ongoing celebration of co-creation.

"What we had *au naturel* in the beginning, we are having to work very hard to recreate in these times when the light has become darkened, when much has been forgotten about how to live in balance on Mother Earth, in consort with all our sisters and brothers from other times and places of harmony among all the elements: air, the Big Mind; delicious and tasty earth, swimming and floating in the waters of Mother's womb; and the purifying fire of spirit to keep us from the worst mistakes of free will."

The portal went as far into the Higher Realms as anyone wanted to go. Because there was little sense of striving, even those who intended to reach the Most High found themselves at some point satisfied, satiated with Holy Magnificence and feeling appropriately ready to descend with their full cargo of spiritual gifts and talents.

"To feel sumptuous and ethereal at the same time, so strange. I am Mother's milk to the masses, or at least as many as I can touch," Daphne continued.

As did Aiyana. "How else would we know what's possible after so many years and lifetimes that life has slid down a more painful and brutal path. No more clambering over steep ice. We will sail in air ships upon the magnetism that flows between us all."

"We are so connected," Atsa added.

And Wu summarized. "We easily confirm the truth we have seen."

Often in their dance there would be a sensation of being totally enfolded in the wings of Isis/personal guardian angel/a lover who truly loves and admires you. Many women and men would experience this simultaneously without seeing or hearing anything, just the touch of an angel in a gigantic downy embrace.

There was another strange phenomenon. Ethereal angels on earth would partially take on the bodies of animals. Some totally turned into dragons and then turned back with smiles on their angelic faces. Tails and hooves and horns proliferated but only on a temporary basis, like putting on a costume for a stage show. It never felt like anyone was really in charge. It certainly never felt that anyone was taking advantage of anyone. Each individual's free will served to combine like elective affinities to produce a more beautiful greater whole.

The ceremony was timeless, and yet at some point it did begin to wind down. The tunnel began to shrink and fade away. All participants began to come back to Earth, knowing they carried everything else with them as they continued their adventurous experiment living primarily in Earth Realm. Aiyana, Atsa, Daphne and Wu felt thoroughly renewed for the work that lay ahead, to manifest again the portal to the Higher Realms that all human beings who wished might regain their birthright and know their ability to travel between worlds, to shape-shift and most importantly to love without reserve.

They were becoming regular observers of the daily life of Turtle Island, loving and learning as they went about these ancient ancestors who seemed to live with grace and dignity and balance pervaded by natural ease. Their ongoing question, how to bring this into the modern world in a time of profound transition?

They found themselves at what looked like some kind of council. The visitors could not understand the words but got the sense that something important was up for discussion. The men and women all talked with gentility and peacefulness that provided a pleasant energetic flow to the proceedings. It also became obvious that the men deferred to the women and that they simply adored them and the women returned that adoration. It was the love of parent and child but also the love and respect of approximate equals. As with everything else in this world, nothing remained fixed. All was waves of deliciously gushing flux. And yet somehow business was being accomplished; discussion was happening; decisions were being made, or rather the music of the discussion brought forth some inevitable conclusion.

The visitors noticed occasionally someone would seem to

lose their immersion in the Flow. Whoever was near and noticed would reach out to reconnect through physical touch. No part of the body was taboo but the touching was extremely light like they were practicing Reiki with one another. The visitors could feel the surge of pleasure accompanying these reconnections. Wu thought, "This feels like the best tantra ever."

"Like being massaged by feathers," Daphne acknowledged.

The visitors found themselves drawn in another direction. The terrain felt increasingly familiar. They still had no relativity regarding what era they might have dropped into, but the feeling was that only years, not centuries had elapsed since the birth of Turtle Island. They recognized the altar of Mother Goddess. They had participated in a ceremony here once before. They felt the tenor and texture of that deeply loving ceremony, where Goddess had appeared like one of them, hardly different from the humans she was among. Certainly, she had a radiance and a certain something which affected all who were touched by her aura. Otherwise, she could have passed for one of the Earth People.

As they came near to the epicenter of Turtle Island, they saw a gigantic figure lying upon and blending with the earth. She was the shape of a woman yet so immense they were awestruck. She appeared to be, and in fact she was, breathing. The rise and fall of her chest, her breasts, each a perfect conical hill, yes, she was a living breathing Goddess. There seemed to be no prohibition to approach her, so they did, coming from the direction of her widely separated feet and legs.

It was as if they had entered a canyon. The walls in color and texture were somewhere between rich brown earth and smooth luscious, tanned skin. She was the ultimate beauty in human form, but also simply a projection from her larger Self, Turtle Island. They were fascinated, of course, as they came closer to her Holy of Holies. This entrée, this deep-throated flower of voluminous velvety yet fleshly petals, where did it lead?

They were unalterably drawn to this ingress, the beginning of a mystery they were yet to fathom. Holding hands, glancing briefly into each other's eyes, with an unspoken assent they slowly approached until they were nudging against the first set of lips. Some intuition led them to softly stroke these pink flamingo lips. As they did so the lips slowly spread and became slicker so that soon they were able to slip inside, an area of deepening pink. They continued to stroke the walls all around them, and the walls continued to loosen and expand, so that they were more easily pulled deeper and deeper inside.

It seemed that they were held just tightly enough even though they were a bit squashed together. There was simultaneously a feeling of unlimited space and time. An infinite universe was open-ended and easily traversed. The lips and mounds became more like clouds, warm and moist and puffy. And eventually they did emerge into a realm of air and air beings. Having gone through a portal, this realm was recognized as a place that was composed more purely of air and liquid light.

They lost all track of time. Later none of them could be sure how long they had danced and cavorted with the sylphs and angels, who felt like old friends. In the Air Realm there was an atmosphere of ongoing celebration with anything being a worthy cause for revelry.

Eventually they returned the way they had come. The final portion of the journey felt very much like being squeezed from a birth canal, and then, there they were again on Turtle Island. In reverence they slowly made their way from between Mother's legs, walked around her, reaching out to touch, trailing their fingers along her flanks and mounds and navigating the thicket of her hair. They returned once again to the magnificent lips that marked the opening of her two-way birth ca-

nal. They kissed her in awe and admiration and almost immediately felt themselves moving through time and space to rejoin the modern Earth World, carrying with them new confir-
mations of imperishable truths.

Visitations and Ruminations

It was a world that I wanted to record because
it was such a miracle visitation to me.
~ Laurie Lee

Thus began regular visits to Turtle Island and one particular village. Zephyr was often their guide and gradually taught the four friends the art of time travel. They were observers in the village, each of them inhabiting the body and mind of one of the villagers without appreciably affecting their daily life or interactions with other villagers.

Their next journey seemed to have taken them several centuries ahead in time. There was a greater abundance of cultivated gardens and less wildness immediately surrounding the village. Still the deer wandered among the village gardens. It seemed they could eat as much as they wanted, and there was still an abundance for the humans. A cornucopia of earthly delights sprang from the fertility of Mother Earth, who continued to walk among them, sometimes openly, sometimes surreptitiously.

The ceremonies to honor her and commune with her had become even more grand. They were times of celebration full of dance and expressions of affection. Truly a garden of earthly delights, the village chugged along to the tune of a pervasive harmony which provided a design much like a mandala. Every piece seemed to fit with every other piece to provide a beautiful awe-inspiring design always present in the foreground or background of daily life. Villagers often had their hands in the rich soil of the place as if they were stroking the body of their Mother Earth, and she responded by giving birth to the bounty that was always there.

Two of the shape-shifting sisters were living on the edge of the village where the order of village life faded into the order of wild nature. Apparently they had been part of the community for many years. In the ensuing years they would be known as shamans. For the time being they were simply known and treated as elder sisters. They shared with the villagers some of their more ancient lore. A few children were drawn to them and became their students or apprentices, learning about shape-shifting, magical flight, healing and other forms of medicine.

In these times only occasionally was there a need for medicine, but it did happen. The four friends were resident observers in the minds of these students when an injured person was brought to the two sisters. They performed a healing ceremony which began with a circle of singers, the four apprentices, several of her friends and the two sisters. Zephyr maintained her invisibility but lent her voice to the shaman's song. The young woman had been running with her friends in one of the wild meadows and had tripped and fallen.

As the singing proceeded, the bleeding from her wound gradually subsided. Then the two sisters placed their hands a few inches above the wound. Everyone else faced their palms toward the woman whose face had gone from pained to almost beatific as the small circle sang to her soul. The four friends could see the flow of energized light that streamed from the palms of all, most intensively from the two sisters. As they watched, the wound healed over and closed and within a few minutes showed no trace of injury.

They learned that what they had witnessed was an integral part of daily life. The medicine women were cohesive members of the community mandala. In these early times the need for such medicine did not arise often, but as the community grew, accidents did happen. These sisters of the Holy Isles had a particular role in the ceremonies which happened often as an affirmation of their position near the center of the mandala to bolster and express the ecstasy of being alive and being the children of Mother Earth, who was still sometimes referred to as Turtle Mother.

Clearly it was the sensuality of running their fingers through the rich steamy earth, the aroma of something so alive. They ate only what they grew, no killing and eating of animals, so even potential predators stayed in their own world. It was part of the protection left behind by the spirit beings who birthed them here from Turtle Mother.

They were preparing for a grand ceremony, the big one of the year. Their new friends actually floated from place to place, and Aiyana had felt her feet leave the ground a few times. Their new friends were constantly morphing. Sometimes they were four birds or little Zephyrs or different Goddesses. They skipped about rather carefree. It was infectious. Even Wu felt lighter and younger, a freshly-minted lotus flower radiant in a pond of moonlight.

One of the four led Atsa away, but everyone soon followed and saw Atsa as a butterfly fluttering with another butterfly. Aiyana thought he looked lovely as a butterfly. She stood as an antelope, seeing all, taking all in. Gleaming over the horizon on the other side of Grandmother Turtle's perfectly round shell mound was the setting sun. On the opposite horizon was the rising full moon, as they entered the shell made of shells built over centuries in this same place. Mollusk shells awash on the nearby beach securely fastened to one another, fashioning something more like a grand arena with an outlandish sense of spaciousness once they were inside.

From all sides the ground sloped toward a hole in the very center. "Worm hole," Atsa's companion joked. "You can call me Alfie. I wanted to be Alpha 'cause I am the firstborn, but people said it was too pretentious. As you have seen, I am always changing. We all are."

"Will we be like that?"

"Not so much. We've been this way since birth."

"So you're related."

"Oh yes, identical quadruplets. Quite rare."

"How long have you been here at this location?"

"Hundreds of years, maybe thousands."

Atsa laughed, practically guffawed.

"Oh, you mean in New Mexico. You see we go back and forth a lot. Not always the same time period on Turtle Island. Part of the story on why we're always morphing, always in transition. We are the epitome of impermanence. We were recognized mainly as time travelers when we first came here. Teachers have come as we've been ready for them. I haven't heard if you have a specialty."

"Not that I've been told."

The whole interchange had the feel of two slightly rascally teenagers cutting it up a little bit at church, but also getting to know each other in the process. Wu oversaw the whole banter and chuckled to himself. *The Tao that can be told is not the real Tao.* He was glad there was room for irreverence right alongside all the reverence.

"Yeah," Alfie responded as if reading his mind. "We make fun of the things we hold most dear. Seems like a good balance. You know, keeps things loose. Keeps us on our toes." He performed a little tiptoe dance to punctuate his message.

"Free will, that was the wild card, the one thing that was not predictable, and look at all the crazy things people will do. Curiosity, wonder what'll happen if I?" Another of the quadruplets was speaking with Wu.

"To do it the other way just to see what happens?"

"That's painful proposition."

"Often it is."

"But that wasn't the first deviation."

"Oh no, the first deviation, lovely topic."

"Advantage, seriously taking advantage."

"Why?" Wu genuinely asked. He had his own thoughts but really wondered what the prevailing view was with these folks.

"It was a different texture of feeling. Fascination with the raw, wild, unpredictable. Maybe something will happen that hasn't happened before."

"I'm trying to understand the fascination."

"It was very small deviations, incremental, but over thousands of years assumptions and instincts changed, so much that the Golden Age has to be somebody's fairy tale pipe dream, not anything approaching true history."

"See you there." Wu concluded with a grin.

The atmosphere was casual, almost careless, certainly carefree as the four friends, the quadruplets, Zephyr and a near equal number of villagers milled about the inside of the turtle shell fashioned out of the remains of the shellfish from the ocean which surrounded Turtle Island.

As if there had been a signal, suddenly the arena became quiet, and Zephyr stated simply, "Now we begin," and soft humming/chanting began. The vowel sounds of all languages were set to a simple melody. "Ah, ay, ee, ai, oh, oo; ah, ay, ee, ai, oh, oo." As the chanting continued, the group in a loose circle sidestepped slowly together. A drumbeat arose from somewhere, perhaps from the hole in the earth at the center of their circle.

Daphne felt herself begin to float off the earth. Looking around she could see that the entire group was now describing a circle in the air. Daphne felt like she was holding hands, but her eyes told her that each person had several feet of separation from those closest to her. The felt connection had to be some form of energy, she concluded, elicited by the ceremony and magnified by their efforts.

A being emerged from the hole, ethereal and even insubstantial at first. She slowly assumed the shape of a matronly but alluring woman. "How can she be both?" Daphne thought, but there was little time for such reflections. The woman was speaking.

"This earth upon which you dwell is my body. The image you see is projected by my universal mind. You are welcome to consciously be with me however you prefer. Because I am constantly giving birth, there are many openings connecting my insides with my outsides. Sometimes these are called places of emergence. For me each one is a birth canal. All that lives is born of me. All of you are always welcome to return to source, to repose for a while in the infinite womb of time and know directly how nurtured you always are."

As they watched, this female figure slowly morphed from one version of divinity to another and another. They were all quite appealing, each one the favorite of someone, who would identify with or seek to merge with. To each individual eye some were ravishing, while others emanated a sedate and stately grace. From siren to Holy Mother, she was winsome to all, and her invitation struck a chord of harmonious yearning for union with that which is most sacred.

"Each of you may return here and enter this birth canal and commune with your inner truth/inner self that you may have this blessed experience of oneness as often as you need or desire." With that the woman ceased her morphing and began to dissolve into a cloud and be drawn back into the opening to the birth canal.

Daphne remembered that she had been on this journey into the womb of the earth, in particular just how blissful it had been to be inside in the presence of the Holy Mother/the Great Mother. How intimate! How delightful!

Wu and Daphne continued to have time together to wander the high desert, to sit in the sunshine wrapped around each other and rapt in each other's presence. Aiyana and Atsa were following a similar path with each other. Their youthful playfulness sustained them as much as the holy ground they walked on and the holy air they inhaled deep within their souls and their collective soul. The felt level of communion in this place just walking about doing nothing special was an ever-present phenomenon.

Zephyr floated in and out of their lives as did the quadruplets. The rest of the community they mostly saw on their visits to Turtle Island, old souls indeed. Their visits were hardly ever disruptive of the daily rhythm of the village. They were not treated as particularly extraordinary. Time travel was fairly common, and there seemed to be no qualms about disrupting the timeline or rewriting history.

"Happens all the time," one of the villagers remarked. "Time, the fourth dimension, right? Usually the changes are small or seem to be small because in the moment we don't remember it being different. It is as it is right now."

"The zen moment," Wu observed.

"Part of our timeline is that the timeline might change, but like I say, it usually doesn't change in big ways. There are actually beings who hold the cohesiveness. Otherwise things would become too fragmented."

"You mean like Chronos?"

"Or Maya. You know the stories in India of the great teachers who would appear in places far distant from each other. Here on Turtle Island your visits from the future are simply part of our reality, as tangible to us as electricity is to you. It's not for everyone. It's kind of like a job title, Time Traveler."

Aiyana began a conversation with Daphne. "I really want to know what happened, how we got from that idyllic place that we've seen, to the struggle we are in now."

"It seems that it was a lot of small changes over thousands of years. It was not some cataclysmic change all at once. No, it was almost imperceptible. It was mostly imperceptible. We recognize it today, the thrill of being a little bit bad."

"Really, something that trivial?"

"Look, it's not so clear cut. We can extrapolate. Remember, 'the thrill of victory, the agony of defeat'. Going for the intense highs and lows, not cruising on a lily pad."

"Okay, I get that but the meanness, the cruelty, competition, one-upmanship."

"It was never supposed to be more than a game, this competition thing. Two couples playing bridge. The Olympics being reinvented was moving away from the dead seriousness of war and back in the direction of friendly competition."

"No original sin, no God, the punisher?"

"Remember that story about how the Brits introduced soccer to the aborigines in Australia, but it proved rather frustrating to the Brits. If one team got too far ahead, they'd slack off and let the other team catch up. They were still living in the dreamtime where that's just what you did."

"They relied for their survival on a matrix of cooperation. Anything that threatened their well-being, if not their survival."

"So there are people living in the old ways right down into modern times."

"Less and less."

"Maybe—look at these folks we've fallen in with, who are telling us there are more like them, hidden away in various remote parts of earth with cloaks of invisibility."

"That still just knocks me over," Aiyana exclaimed.

"We were kinda prepared...you know Grandmother Xochitl's camp. We've all been traveling in the other world."

"Now we're seeing more of the network, the history, our place in it all."

"Yeah, we have a place."

"Do we ever..."

"I hope we actually get more of the story from Turtle Island till now."

"That's a lot."

"I wanna know the details, you know, vignettes to signify how those incremental changes happened."

"Some of that might be possible."

"We could fly away to key transition points and be flies on the wall."

"I wanna be a dragonfly."

"I reckon that they're going to try to give the most relevant pieces for whatever work we're destined for."

After a lull in the conversation, Aiyana asked, "Could I sit with you like you do with Wu?"

Daphne did not answer immediately but sat with the question and others such as, "Is this part of my truth, right now." She looked up and met the eyes of Aiyana. "Yes, I think that would be lovely. My lap or yours?"

In answer Aiyana scooched next to Daphne and dramatically slung one leg around the other woman's waist. Daphne giggled at the childlike playfulness of her friend. Thus they rested comfortably in each other's arms for much of the afternoon.

"There was a time when I wanted to be rich and powerful."

"Really?" Aiyana exclaimed.

"Yeah," Atsa acknowledged. "I would go to my aunt's house in town and see these things on TV, and I would want them. They were shiny. They were glitzy, colorful."

"Yeah, I guess I kinda get that. You were really young, right? I didn't see any of that stuff till I went to school. When I was really young, I was with my mother or my grandmother and the sheep and learning to weave."

"I think we dream and daydream whatever seemed attractive when we were little people."

"I know you know this now. When you're out on the land your vision is big and wide, like it is now out here on this magic land. Why put your vision in a box, a facsimile of what is, but not really what is?"

"For people in cities it's a step up. I really get it. I saw a very pretty picture of a little girl, you, with the sheep. I wanted to be there."

"So you understand the temptation to be rich and powerful, to have all the glitzy toys in a material world."

"I did understand that at one time. Now it's hard to relate to. It's so harsh. We have lived with the threat of something terrible happening for many generations."

"We are learning about these other beings, the Hidden Ones. They are here to help us as much as they can, help us trace our minds back to Source, that oneness with Mother on the most cosmic level. Changing Woman, we know her, and by many other names."

"She is Mother Earth, and she wraps Mother Earth in her protection, she whose breath is the Milky Way and galaxies beyond."

"And each one of us, female and male, equally eligible to

know her joy."

"Mother Turtle of Turtle Island, where we danced through the air in her temple shell made of shells."

"The lovely intimacy of those we've been close to. The awe-inspiring vastness of the Cosmic Mothers."

"Of Universal Mind," Atsa added.

"We are completing each other's poetic lines."

"We are complementary elements."

"Elective affinities."

"Ooh, I like the sound of that. What are they?"

She became very professorial in tone. "Elective affinities describes two chemicals that are in solution with many other chemicals, but these two chemicals will always gravitate toward each other over and above all others."

"I elect to be with you. You elect to be with me."

"There's a word for groups that gather in the same way, but I can't remember it."

"Us with Wu and Daphne might be one of those."

"We're certainly all drawn to one another."

"Maybe it's just family in the truest sense of the word."

"You have a way of breaking things down to their simplicity. Sometimes I get lost in minutiae."

"I don't think it's minutiae. You just like the gory details."

"Oh, that makes it so much better." Her voice was dripping with irony.

"Sometimes you tell complex stories. I like them. Sometimes I love them. I suspect if we're supposed to teach the story of Turtle Island, you'll be great at it."

"Thank you. I love you, Atsa," she said in Navajo. He looked at her and silently mouthed the same words in response.

They sat for a while with a warm sun to their backs, gazing into the distance, watching the subtle changes in color from the angle of the sun. There seemed to be much more pink than usual. They knew how to feel each other while sitting side by side. Today felt particularly wonderful, not needing anything extra to make it fabulous.

They felt themselves floating up and away while maintaining a comfortable cross-legged posture. They were awash in colorful designs above and around them. They'd seen these designs on rugs and blankets and ponchos. Far below they could see where they'd been sitting and the flatlands, canyons and mountains that receded into the distance. They could see the highway and the access road they had taken to their little village. A plume of dust rose from that road. Someone was coming. This had not happened since they had been there, so far as they knew.

They were drawn to the village and felt themselves descending until they found themselves standing quietly at the edge of the activity generated by the arrival of a woman and a man in caked-with-dust SUV. At first Atsa and Aiyana heard, "We need a healer."

Zephyr had met the new arrivals and replied, "Of course. Can we also send along our four apprentices? Kind of a training mission, but they are already quite talented."

"The more singers the better, right?"

"Tinkering, trying some apparent improvement, like modern science and the way it's been used have brought us to the brink of planetary disaster." Daphne was talking, and Wu was occasionally nodding or grunting as if in agreement.

"Failure of compassion," Wu offered. Daphne looked at him expectantly. "Something happened, something worse than usual disaster. Before that everything was shared. What's yours is mine. What's mine is yours. I am you, and you are me. Competition for survival among earth people happened for the first time."

"There had to be a first time. First time for all the experiments that didn't turn out so well. Didn't like that there were events that caused miseries. So maybe that was the grand experiment; how will the children of the Garden handle adversity. That's the knowledge of good and evil, so to speak, but it's not really evil; it's just adversity. But some people are evil."

"That comes later, much later."

"So at first it's just dealing with things being less than ideal. Think of all the adversity we cope with now: diseases, natural disasters, crop failures, and the bad reactions of other humans."

"It's amazing we're not at war all the time," Wu observed.

"That was a big leap: 'Wars and rumors of wars.' 'Life out of balance.' This incremental process of doing something that takes advantage of someone else, a little minor cheating, but it escalates over time."

"Yes, until here we are on the edge of quite a nightmare, if all the predicted disasters happen at once. Must be why we're here relearning how to walk between the worlds."

"No solution without the gifts of spirit. Science alone cannot solve the problems. They're too big."

"So some of us will live underground again, and some of us will fly away with the angels and sylphs."

"Some will be in suspended animation awaiting the new heavens and new earth," Daphne concluded.

Just then Zephyr broke in on their conversation, and they accompanied her to the newcomers who had come in search of a healing.

Balance

I am Shakti, as well as Shiva. I am everything male
and female, light and dark, flesh and spirit. Perfectly balanced
in one single moment lasting an eternity.
~ Robin Rumi

Only when Shiva is united with Shakti
does he have the power to create.
~ Soundarya

There was a sense of urgency, something the four friends had not experienced much in their travels. Gordon drove the SUV and Mary rode in the jeep with Atsa, Aiyana and Zephyr. It was somewhat jarring to be suddenly thrust so totally into the stricter contingencies of the physical plane. The story unfolded as they drove as fast as they could on poor quality country roads. Zephyr explained, "When we are here on the physical plane, we have to play by the rules...most of the time. I gather from Mary and George that there has been an injury, fairly serious. Time is of the essence."

Just then a coyote ran across the road from left to right. Zephyr's focus shifted to the coyote, watching it disappear and then closing her eyes. Her lips were moving as if she were mumbling something, but there was no sound.

Soon she returned. "I think it's going to be all right. They're already getting it under control, but it's good we're going. There's some trauma. Gordon must know. He's slowed down a little."

Another side road full of ruts and bumps brought them to a hogan with a house trailer and pick-up truck nearby. An older boy lay underneath a canopy, with one leg exposed but already wrapped in some moist leafy herbs. The woman kneeling beside him spoke. "We already gave him *osha*. He's still really out of it, not here."

Zephyr laid a hand on her shoulder. "Let's get right to work." She motioned to the group. They sat in a circle around the boy and laid their hands on him. Zephyr began a simple song. Soon everyone had joined in and were singing with her and in harmony with her. A soft drumbeat entered the circle of sound. Another boy stood a few feet away with a handsomely painted hand drum.

Wu was drawn to hold his hand above the injured boy's heart. He could feel the *chi* flowing from his hand into the boy's heart center and then to the rest of his body, particularly the area where the poison had been injected by the snake.

Milo, the boy, was in a dream world where he had been swallowed by a gigantic snake, but he was also the snake. He was dissolving only to become himself. When he had thoroughly digested himself, he turned into a dragon and flew over the countryside including the place where his body lay under the ministering hands of the eight directions. From where he soared in the sky, he belched a breath of fire to his boy self who lay unconscious on a blanket in the sand. He circled lower and belched again. Two more times he circled ever lower and belched his fire before circling higher and higher into the heavens and disappearing.

The boy's consciousness had returned to the boy. He was not yet awake, but everyone felt his life returning to him and inwardly rejoiced as they continued to sing and channel the energy of life into him and through him. They also began to look around and smile at one another in between their longer moments of serious focus. They were on the home stretch.

Milo's awakening was gradual. His eyelids fluttered, opened, closed again. He experienced himself resting in a warm bath of golden light, which flowed through him and suffused his entire being. He was content to float and let the pleasant sensations increase his joy and well-being. When he did open his eyes and keep them open, there was a golden radiance around the circle of hands and eyes he initially noticed. He was further fulfilled by their obvious love and felt himself responding with his own radiance, a circulation of golden light that included him.

A part of Milo started to float away from his body and hovered a few feet in the air. He looked at it and called it back, thinking, "I don't think I'm ready for that."

Arms were extended to welcome the drummer into the circle. The younger brother almost fell on Milo and hugged him as hard as he could. Milo hugged him back. Both had tears in their eyes.

Some eyes rested on the mother, who sat back and closed her eyes, mouthing silent prayers of gratitude, letting go of the fear and adrenaline. Zephyr and Mary moved to either side of her and gently held her. Naomi felt their love and healing touch and relaxed into herself.

Milo sat with his little brother, the drummer. He felt very light-headed but otherwise no worse for wear. Obviously these folks knew about the village devoted to medicine teachings where the group had just come from, but did not live there themselves. As if in answer to an unspoken question, Gordon suddenly but quietly spoke. "Yes, we live dispersed as we always have. We are among those who live in the world between worlds." He nodded toward Milo. "Not always so skillful at how we negotiate the physical world. Better when we're flying through star systems. Up there we have more helpers. Space is not empty. It's full of beings. They are the beings of air. We are the beings of earth. Turtle Island was born from the realm where the water beings live."

"We're always in school here," Daphne thought.

"Yes, purple dragon type beings who fly through the stratosphere trailing purple fire."

Atsa was shocked that Gordon had seen right into his mind, and he thought he was just looking at some animé character.

"Such beings exist in the vast reaches of the heavens, among the many who are primarily composed of air. The purple dragons are quite friendly and really good dancers."

"So you are a Traveler," Aiyana stated more than asked.

"I've been fortunate to have positions that required a lot of deep space travel. It's an advanced form of shape-shifting. Some of you have traveled through space on the coattails of other beings, so to speak. Wu, your travels with Toloache were quite profound and far-reaching. You've all traveled through time. Some of you have been to the womb of Mother Earth." He looked at Daphne.

"Who is this person," she thought.

"Mary and I do our best to look like late middle-age retirees, slightly overweight, cruising around in our 5th wheel. We really like the Southwest, land of enchantment." He laughed. "Turns out to be true. Your friends have a settlement. Mmm, Calabasas?"

"You just pick things out of people's minds, don't you?" Daphne queried.

"As soon as you thought it, I knew it. Your friends are creating a portal with the air beings."

"They were when we left."

"How long have you been gone... Oh, two years."

"Stop that."

"Okay, two years is a long time."

"Yes, we're on our way there now. For two years we did not feel called back."

"And now?"

"Still not a sense of urgency. Important to be going that direction. Clearly we've taken quite a side-trip here."

"This is your preparation. You are called back to Calabasas to bring with you the wisdom and knowledge that you're gaining here."

"Are you overseeing our mission?"

"You could say that, one of many guides, teachers, ascended masters."

They both laughed. Daphne simultaneously had a vision of a blue god, like Krishna perhaps, sitting cross-legged on a silken throne, surrounded by deer, birds, and other wildlife. There was a sweet aroma of gardenias, and she just adored this blue god.

Her eyes arose to meet Gordon's mischievous grin. All he said was, "I adore him too."

Later in the day Gordon approached Wu. "Your mind is rather empty," he observed.

"Thank you," Wu replied.

"You could be a Traveler, if you wanted to be."

"I travel now."

"You know what I mean."

Wu chuckled and replied, "I do not seek change, but things never remain the same... Why me?"

"You already have a disciplined mind. That is somewhat rare in modern times."

"What would that mean for me?"

"You would remain here longer than your friends."

"And Daphne?"

"She has important work in Calabasas."

Wu rested deeply in No-Mind for a few minutes before knowing what he wished to say. "We have been such good partners."

"And you will be again."

"Do you see everything so clearly?"

"Only when it's important for me to see."

"But earlier with Daphne?"

"I was just playing around, showing off, having some fun with her. It's easy to get into these roles and take ourselves way too seriously."

"Your humor helps me to trust you."

"And what causes distrust... my appearance?"

Wu burst out laughing. "Probably," he finally managed to say.

"How about if I looked like this?" In a few seconds, Gordon morphed into a rather perfect image of a Taoist Immortal.

Instinctively Wu enclosed one fist in the other hand and bowed to the mentor of all mentors. He stood with his hands clasped and asked, "So you've been messing with me this whole time?"

"We are called upon to play at various levels in many different domains. Often we assume a form that will elicit the greatest receptivity in our audience."

"Are you truly one of the Immortals?"

"I am in enough harmony with that spirit to sometimes take it on. It's possible that you could soon have that ability."

Gordon was building a good case for Wu staying on longer at the village between the worlds. He was not particularly surprised by the turn of events. His teacher had always said, "Truth is truth. Wisdom is wisdom. It does not matter who says it or what tradition they espouse."

"In this world between worlds all wisdom-traditions have a voice," he thought. He looked at Gordon, the Taoist Immortal, and knew he wanted to know more of the story, particularly how the tradition he'd been following, fit into the greater picture. As he was looking, Gordon and the Immortal separated but were superimposed on each other. The incongruous nature of the blended image sparked Wu into another fit of laughter. He reflected that he had not laughed like this in years.

Then he was again looking at Gordon, the paunchy middle-aged American tourist on his way to the next trailer park or campground. He bowed to him with the same respect and reverence as when Gordon had looked like, or had been, the Taoist Immortal. Wu looked him in the eye, grinned and stated simply, "I guess you've got a deal."

"Mary and I will soon be coming to stay at your village for a while. First, we have some things to complete here."

The next days were devoted to preparations for taking leave of this magical village where they had been shown so much. Wu and Daphne had been relatively inseparable for the last couple of years. Now Daphne would proceed with Atsa and Aiyana, and Wu would remain behind. There were reassurances from Zephyr and others that they would be reunited in the not-too-distant future. They both had been practicing a level of detachment for some time, but they had definitely gotten used to each other's presence and support.

When not involved in further training, they wandered the high desert together and sat for long periods in yab-yum or yum-yab, enclosing each other in mindful presence and bodily quiescence. Their beings were slowly adjusting to an altered future.

On the day of departure, the four were invited to sit in four camp chairs. Wu was somewhat distant from the other three. Their new friends, classmates and teachers were all dressed in full pow-wow regalia. A unified rhythm was provided by drums and rattles. Zephyr came to each of them individually, surrounded them with sage smoke, prayed over them in one of her many languages and brushed their bodies and auras with the eagle feathers of an ornately beaded fan.

All of them felt uplifted, cleared of lingering doubts and anxieties and ready for the next act, whatever it brought to each of them. The group joined together in a farewell song, which was hauntingly familiar, but the soon-to-be travelers and Wu could not identify it and concluded it must be from one of the ancient places they had recently visited. Each of the three travelers received a farewell hug from everyone present, and Zephyr kissed them on both cheeks.

Zephyr accompanied them to Atsa's jeep and added her personal farewell. "You remain with us, and we go with you. We are blessed, and we will meet again in this world or the other one."

Except for the recent healing excursion, they had not been on a highway in several months. They were many miles from Calabasas, their most immediate destination. Daphne thought of her friends there. She had not seen them in more than two years. She and Wu had been called to wander just as the folks at Calabasas were beginning their collaboration with the air beings. Daphne had meanwhile descended into the womb of the earth and gained profound understandings of how the underground realm is as spiritual and supportive of earth people as the heavenly realm is.

Atsa had gotten them to the magical village, which still remained nameless. As a point of reference, they began to refer to it as Zephyr's place. Now Daphne would direct them to Calabasas. Aiyana was being drawn there by an energy that she certainly could feel in her body and could almost see. As the youngest of the three and given all that she had learned and been exposed to in her young life, she exuded a delightful openness often found only in the very young, who have not lost their connection to the other world. She'd had the good fortune to be recognized as special at an early age and provided with experiences and techniques to maintain that connection.

Aiyana knew she was on the threshold of another immersion in otherworldly wisdom and could feel her excitement as they proceeded toward Calabasas. Atsa felt himself quite gifted to be traveling with these two magical women and was proud to be their chauffeur.

Within a few days Gordon and Mary arrived at the village,

towing their house trailer. Wu had little contact with Mary, but Gordon became a recurrent presence and clearly had arrived to be his teacher. After so many female teachers it was odd, a bit jarring even, to have a teacher assuming such an off-putting male persona.

Gordon heard his thought, of course. "Would you like me better if I was more attractive?" For a few seconds he seemed to become Rita Hayworth, bombshell actress of another era. Then he laughed as he became Gordon again. "I represent your worst prejudice, don't I?" He guffawed. "Good old boy, kinda rough around the edges, white, unaware. How am I doing?" He slapped Wu lightly on the shoulder.

"You're right. Wisdom doesn't look like you."

Gordon chortled this time and declared, "Good for you that you admitted it so readily. We can move right along. You will laugh when I tell you the main thrust of our studies."

Wu waited and seemed to stare off in the distance. He even began to whistle.

"That's the spirit." Gordon broke into his pretense of reverie. "Okay, I'm going to drop the ugly American act with you, but I have some reasons for maintaining it with the other students. Zephyr knows, of course. She's a shape-shifter, too."

They had been walking and talking, leaving the village far behind. "Let's sit," Gordon suggested. As he descended to earth, his Bermuda shorts and Hawaiian shirt dissolved and were replaced by robes similar to Wu's. His body also changed, becoming smaller, slimmer and decidedly androgynous.

Both sat quietly contemplating the fluctuating colors of the distant mountains and sky. When Gordon next spoke it was without the brash bravado that he had steadily portrayed up until then. His tone was quiet and measured, seeming to Wu to be speaking with the voice of Wu's mind. "You already know that we are all fundamentally female. Male traits were a later invention. Maleness can be entertaining in small doses. When I flooded you with my maleness, you found me obnoxious. So we know all this. How do we communicate to the average guy out there, who believes he really is male and feels very threatened at the suggestion that he might be anything but pure male?"

"In ancient times we knew better. What happened? What caused us to forget, another failed experiment?"

"There was some curiosity whether the cultivated ultramale could on his own find his way back to his feminine core essence."

"Possible, not likely, I'm guessing. So how?"

"The children who are about to be born will understand how fluid and transitory gender can be. Their parents must find a way to validate their journey. They must not try to force them back into rigid structures and definitions. These souls know that gender is irrelevant to spirit."

"So we have a mission, and our mission is to prevent these parents from destroying their children."

"To put it bluntly." There was a long silence, before Gordon turned to Wu and with a great deal of warmth declared, "I look forward to working with you."

"Likewise."

Later on they continued.

"How important do you think it is, this conscious recognition of our own femaleness?"

"You can say femininity if you want," Gordon countered.

"I acknowledge that is more the thing that we men shy away from."

"Even you?"

"You have not met macho wandering Taoist?"

"Lurking about?"

Wu declared, "So much of our practice is a push away from that out-of-balance foundation of the modern world."

"Many centuries of brutal warriors wailing away at each other and the women and the children."

"Can we recall ourselves? Can we reclaim ourselves? Are those even the right questions?"

"You will discover how much power you have to make good choices, but you already know that. Look at how you've lived your life."

"Macho deprivation, macho living on the edge, Macho Mindful Man, he's a superhero."

"You're really pulling my leg now, aren't you?"

"Just trying to play in the band."

Gordon chuckled. "You are."

Again they were walking beyond the village where things felt more wild and alive. They often saw critters. Today was a rabbit, as they continued to explore their own softness.

"The brighter male principle should always place itself below the darker, softer feminine principle to achieve and maintain balance."

"If the feminine principle were somehow seen as stronger, it would be an easier sell."

"We shouldn't have to sell anything," Wu responded.

"This is America."

"Mother Earth."

"Okay."

"Seriously, all of our lessons out here in the Land of Enchantment have been about the power and primacy of Mother Earth. The best we get to do is be her children."

"We gotta get graphic, require men to be involved in childbirth, just be present. Figure it out. How a brother is also a sister. To be able to be both. To prepare at least some men to experience what we've experienced, or have you? As a woman I've traveled in her birth canal. I've been to her womb and back. That's ahead of you. Once you've been there, there's no denying the power of the feminine."

"Hallelujah, sister or brother or holy sib."

"So this is the monkish reserve that you carry around?"

"It's important to maintain, like your good old boy middle American. But it's fun to come out and play once in a while."

"Are you man enough to travel to the center of the earth? Great Mother, Earth Mother wants you on her team."

"Your team got a name?" Wu asked.

"Earth Ecstasy."

"All right! Mother Earth's Ecstasy, you can have some too. She'll carry you away, and you'll love it."

"Shiva cannot exist without Shakti. She always leads in the story of creation."

The Voice of Changing Woman

Now the night will throw its cover down
On me again
~ Norah Jones

Uncharacteristically, they drove for many miles that first day back on the road. Aiyana started out in the front seat with Atsa, but thereafter migrated to the back where she joined Daphne drifting in and out of sleep. When Daphne relieved Atsa behind the wheel, he declared, "Really tired."

"We don't have the energy of the village to sustain us," Aiyana commented before he curled up in her arms and fell into a deep sleep. She adored this young man, who had come into her life and was delighted that among the panoply of feelings she had for him, some were definitely maternal. She was amused at feeling so maternal, not just toward little kids, but also toward this strapping youth who slept peacefully in the circle of her loving arms.

They were fellow travelers on a journey together, a journey of exploration and discovery. So many extraordinary experiences, it certainly felt like they were being prepared for something dramatic, something to help themselves and others move through the coming earth changes with as little grief as possible.

Daphne had been told directly that she had an important role in the coming events. She even felt pushed toward leadership. She had been quite comfortable being not too visible, teaching a handful of people here and there in the shadows or at least the less well-lit places. Perhaps she would remain semi-cloaked but in a more prominent role in an expanded community. "I guess I'll know when I need to know," she murmured to herself. As the miles rolled past, something was shifting inside of her. She was more blithely accepting whatever destiny lay before. She thought about the folks in Calabasas and wondered who would be there. So many pleasant memories drifted through the shimmering landscape of her road-focused mind.

She thought especially of Flor, the telepathic babe in arms, whose messages had already impelled so much singularly focused activity at Calabasas and some other communities. She remembered with pleasure her time with the Goddess Circle in Northern California, her friends and lovers. Where were they all now? What had happened in the more than two years she'd been out of touch? And the Goddess Sanctuaries, the sisters of that group, comrades and comadres in solidarity with all others trying to pave a smooth path into a glorious future; a time of renewal lay ahead, a time of consolidation and creation. Build the infrastructure, educate and invite those who've long yearned for a return to the original visions and understandings of how to live life as a loving community.

"We're part way there," she mused, "with so much still needing to be done." And after a mindful pause. "At least my life has meaning." She laughed at her own joke.

They were apparently out in the middle of nowhere. There was only one poorly maintained sign, ART GALLERY AHEAD. Daphne needed a rest stop anyway. One room was jam-packed with art objects: pottery, paintings, beadwork, wood-carving, rugs and other weavings.

"We are an artist community. We take turns minding the

store." The older man still had jet black hair reaching to his waist.

"Which are your pieces?" Daphne asked.

"I should make you guess, but take your time."

"Okay, but first I need a rest room."

"Anywhere out back you wanna go... Need paper?"

"Thanks."

"Just bring the paper back. You'll see the trash can."

Aiyana and Atsa were tuning into various pieces. Aiyana was drawn to a depiction of Changing Woman, her face in approximate quadrants: blue-gray, tan, cream and red rock, zigzag lines of energy in every direction. A stream flowed from her mouth. Her angles were shocking yet, somehow, she was attractive, alluring and serene.

"Balancing and rebalancing of female and male," the artist offered.

"And transformation," Aiyana softly replied. "Is this yours?"

"And harmony. It is the woman's nature to be ever-changing like the seasons, like the moon cycle. She asked the sun to build her a special house, because it's so important that they work together."

"What is it to be, a man...or a woman?" Atsa thought out loud.

"If we do the ceremonies, the spirits will show us the way."

"We've been experiencing a bit of that." Daphne had returned. "You could say we've entered the ceremonial world."

"How do you like it?"

"We love it," Aiyana gushed.

"At this point I can't imagine being on any other journey—"

"That would even come close." Aiyana finished Atsa's sentence.

"Let me show you my Changing Woman drum. Well, it's not mine, but it might be yours." A little bolt of energy shot out of one eye. He handed the drum and beater to Aiyana. "See how you like the sound."

The resonance of the drum filled the room. Aiyana cruised into a simple rhythm and soon they all heard chanting or singing that was not emanating from any of them.

"Spirit drum." Aiyana looked at the man, who nodded almost imperceptibly.

"I think you've found your drum," Daphne declared.

Aiyana demurred and Daphne restated, "I'm sure of it. I'm going to buy it for you."

"I can't let you. You don't have money."

Daphne smiled. "You gotta keep my secret."

"You're really a rich heiress."

They all laughed before Daphne continued. "Actually no, but I do have an emergency fund that I can write checks off of. You will take a personal check?"

"You tell me it's good; I believe you."

Aiyana had one more question. "Does this qualify as an emergency?"

Daphne laughed. "My guide spirit tells me that you and your drum will be a vital part of something in the not-too-distant future."

"There's one more thing," the drum maker interjected. "I would like you to take a short walk with me. Bring your drum."

Soon after they returned, the travelers departed. They could feel a pleasant warmth following them from the little gallery. "Is it something you can tell us?" Daphne asked.

"There's a personal ceremony I will do to wake up the drum."

"Did the drum maker remind you of Gordon?"

"As soon as you said it..." Atsa began, then realized the question wasn't directed to him.

Aiyana reflected and lightly stroked her drumhead. "I can see that. What do you think that means?"

"We don't know what his limits are," Daphne stated matter-of-factly.

"They or he like being the trickster," Atsa declared.

Within a couple of hours the sun was low on the western horizon. Atsa pulled onto a faint dirt path that lasted only a hundred yards or so before ending in a small wilderness cul-de-sac. An older pick-up truck was already there. Three women sat in a circle together. Aiyana volunteered to talk with the women. Two of them wore the velvet blouses so common in this region. The other was pale-skinned and dressed in a bright cowboy shirt and jeans. For some reason Aiyana carried her drum with her.

"Changing Woman." The woman in the maroon blouse exclaimed.

Aiyana was not totally surprised and replied, "It seems that you know her."

The women exchanged glances with each other and the older woman stepped forward. "May I look at your drum?"

Ordinarily Aiyana might have felt more protective, but for some reason she felt totally safe with this woman. The younger woman began to talk about Changing Woman. "We are on a pilgrimage, a sacred journey in this, the special land of Changing Woman. West of the Sangre de Christo Mountains between a river and a rocky ridge, the Earth-heated waters of Changing Woman rise to the surface and gather in healing pools. Further to the west just beyond the pools lies a place where geology has marked the Four Directions: four high desert plains intersect at a power point. This is a region of origins, a place of birth and beginnings. From this place each year the Journey of Waters begins. We will start there and go on a path that has been followed since ancient times."

Kushala, the older woman, held the drum and asked, "Would you and your friends like to join us. We are eating lightly, but I'm sure we have enough."

"And we can contribute. Thank you so much." She waved

to Daphne and Atsa to join them. A lively discussion ensued. As Kushala continued to cradle Aiyana's drum, the three women talked about Changing Woman as if she were a member of their family.

"Changing Woman is so important in these times of purification and transition."

"She takes people beyond fixed realities to the truth of what is going on, and then into taking action to live out that truth in their daily lives."

"She helps ease people through changes. She helps them to see who they actually are and what actually is."

"Right relationship."

There was a lull and Daphne talked a bit about their mission. "We are working to bring about positive change in these times, to combine the sacred power of Earth Mother with the sacred power of the heavenly beings."

Kushala responded. "The feminine energy is what's going to change the world, not the masculine energy. Actually, it's the feminine combined with masculine energy, the coming together of the two of them that will make a difference."

Aiyana and Atsa looked into each other's eyes, remembering their times of communion through their practice of tantra.

While Aiyana beat her drum softly, the women continued to free associate with Changing Woman, who is Goddess, Sister, Holy Mother and the mother who feeds you and keeps you clean. Their words came in English and several other languages, but everyone seemed to understand everything that was spoken, chanted, and sung.

"Changes continuously."

"Never dies."

"In winter she's an old woman."

"In spring young and vibrant again."

"She is the same woman over and over again."

"Infinite variations."

"White Painted Woman."

"Moon Mother."

"Her house floats on the western waters."

"Where the Sun visits her every day."

"There are children."

"Monster Slayer."

"Child of Water."

"The monsters of our minds washed away by pure water."

Daphne's Taoism fit right in with flow.

"We are made of her skin."

"Where we live."

"What we eat."

"She is everything."

"We are her creations."

"Forever lovingly connected."

"She grew up in four days."

"Medicine bundle gives birth to Beauty."

"Prepare yourself for something that is going to happen; after a while I will visit you." Atsa spoke the words of the sun.

"First wedding for the mating of corn."

"Whistling of wind."

"Feathers of eagle."

"Growth of corn."

"Child of Earth."

"Child of Sky."

"Child of the Sacred Mountains."

"White light of Dawn."

"Blue light of midday."

"Yellow light of twilight."

"Black light of night."

"Wind, air, atmosphere."

"Holy Wind Spirit."

"Each breath a taste of Truth."

"She comes upon me with blessing."

"I have come upon blessing."

"Help us to do our best."

"Correct us when we don't."

The singing continued into the night. The focus gradually shifted to more traditional songs including some country gospel: "Amazing Grace", "Life is Like a Mountain Railway," "You're Drifting Too Far From the Shore." Atsa even sang a Bob Marley song.

For a while the group settled on an old-time music refrain, singing harmonies and flights of fandango:

Oh, come, angel band,
Come and around me stand;
Oh, bear me away on your snow white wings
To my immortal home;
Oh, bear me away on your snow white wings
To my immortal home.

Sometimes an individual would drift away for a while, sometimes returning with blankets or a bottle of water or a bag of dried fruit. The circle of six, seven counting Changing Woman, sang and drummed through the night. The harmony was as if they had known each other all their lives. Another drum appeared with an image of Changing Woman. The drumming never stopped throughout the night with a three-quarter moon casting a silvery glow on the impromptu gathering.

Each group of three held and supported their drummer. They leaned in to one another like two very stable tripods. Coyotes, at times, joined their mutual serenade. Daphne's words to Aiyana reverberated in her own mind: "...you and your drum will be a vital part of something in the not-too-distant future."

The powerful energy, the medicine, of their singing and their physical closeness kept them warm until first light shot a few rays over the horizon. Sunrise songs continued in the mix of languages, including "Here Comes the Sun", "Sun, sun, sun, here it comes", and "Carry On", which felt like a Changing Woman song:

The sky is clearing and the night
Has gone out
The sun, he come, the world
Is all full of love
Rejoice, rejoice, we have no choice
But to carry on

"How do you feel about being a woman for a while?" Gordon asked the question expecting some reaction from Wu. Instead they continued to walk in silence for many minutes. Gordon began to wonder if Wu had heard the question, or maybe he didn't know how he felt. Gordon resisted the temptation to mind read. It was possible he wouldn't have seen anything definitive anyway.

Finally Wu responded. "It's not like I've really thought of myself as a man. As a teenager my manhood was regularly ridiculed. None of my efforts ever made me more masculine to my peers. Then I met my teacher and cared even less about what anybody thought, plus my growing skill at martial arts made the bullying less intimidating. I only had one fight, but after that everybody just left me alone. The kid didn't report me. He was so embarrassed to get his ass kicked by the wimpy kid."

"So, gender identity?"

"Probably neutral."

"I'm proposing that you have an experience of being ultra-feminine."

"I don't even know what that is. I've been around a lot of

women, especially after I began teaching. I think I always looked on them as neutral. I look at everybody as pretty much neutral."

"How about me?"

Wu burst out laughing. "You are a stereotypically obnoxious American male, like a cardboard cut-out."

Gordon laughed. "I've succeeded."

"If that was your goal, you definitely have."

"Let's just start with your body. In time you'll be able to shape-shift and do this for yourself. Right now, with your permission I would like to transform you into a beautiful woman."

"How about an old hag or a young girl? It sounds easier."

"All right, we have plenty of time to explore it all. Tell me when you're ready, and which do you prefer?"

"Now?"

"You have a better time?"

"I guess not... I would like to be a crone. Can I sit and meditate for a few minutes?"

When Wu came out of his meditation, he announced, "I'm ready now." He did feel ready, peaceful with even some positive anticipation.

"Beautiful, stay where you are and close your eyes again."

Wu did as directed. As he returned to his meditative space, he began to feel slow small changes in his body. His external genitals shrank and then disappeared. Saggy breasts grew on his chest. Most profoundly there was a new space in the middle of his abdomen, which was not there before. S/he could feel the potential even though her body was way beyond childbearing. Her womb was alive and ready for new life to happen.

"Okay," Gordon declared. "Just go where you need to go, see what you need to see, feel what you need to feel and know what you need to know."

Old woman Wu sat in a circle with several other old women. They were all in full regalia, as if they had been at a pow-wow or a more sacred ceremony. Judging by the differences in their dress, they came from a variety of intact traditions.

In silence, s/he felt the wisdom of the circle before one of the women began to speak. "We have all been mothers. We are now grandmothers. Each of us comes from an unbroken line that goes back to the time when all women were shamans, and men felt their blessing as they went through their lives in various states of free play. Even though the men were consorts at times, most of the time they were treated as the blessed children that they assuredly were, and they wanted nothing more. Challenges and struggles were only the ones they invented as part of their games."

Another woman took up the commentary: "We are so ancient, we are almost immortal, but in the biological world sometimes we need to discard a body and replace it with one that works better for doing the work. We are repositories for the wisdom of the ages, the wisdom of the cosmos, the wisdom that rises up from the earth. And we know those places to go when we need even greater wisdom. Right now we are poised because this earth plane is on the threshold of some major dramatic changes. Earth people have neglected the voice of the earth, that different language that has guided earthly existence for millennia. Some time ago some men decided they only need listen to the sky god in some form or other. The sky god does not directly nurture biological reality. The voice of Mother Earth is absolutely essential."

A third woman continued the story. "Men tasted power from above and became enamored with it, more enamored than they were with their women and they particularly began to neglect the wise old women, who spoke with the voice of Mother Earth. It started with, 'We don't need their magic.' And then the rallying cry was, 'Their magic is evil.' Rather than understanding the masculine and feminine as complementary pieces of a universal flow, the masculine was exalted and the feminine demeaned. Now those actions and thoughts have brought the biological world to the edge of massive destruction."

Seamlessly the fourth woman talked with almost the same voice. "We don't know what will be left, except we know that Spirit is imperishable, and the biological realm will renew itself. How long that will take, we don't know. Right now we are helping to gather relatively evolved humans to provide a nucleus for what comes next, so that the so-called new heavens and new earth will not go backward in terms of human evolution. All of us are working with one or more of the enclaves around the world so that the transition is ultimately a step forward for the human race on earth."

The fifth woman, who sat to Wu's right, completed the story. "We are gathering allies all the time. The womb wisdom of women knows implicitly how to live in balance. Women are awakening every day. As they awaken, we will be there to join with them, to guide them, to design a future that leaves out nothing important."

After the women's circle, Wu and Gordon sat together in the open air. Wu was still exploring with his mind the old woman's body he was now inhabiting. "I feel really different in this body," he acknowledged to Gordon.

"Tell me," Gordon requested.

"Years of practice as a monk did not get me to where I am now. I learned detachment. I practiced being in the moment. Now I feel a love for all creation, the love of a mother for her children. I never felt this before. Even sitting yab-yum with Daphne simply increased the depth and flow of what I could already do on my own. This is qualitatively different."

"The best of modern religions still leave out Goddess, relationship with Mother Earth. It's the organic connection. She lives in all of us, but we have to acknowledge and, most importantly, experience her, experience that Mother Goddess energy that flows through you, that is you."

"I get that now." Wu reflected for a moment. "How did we get so far off track?"

"In ancient times everyone born in a male body went through an initiation, experiencing themselves in a woman's body so that they wouldn't forget that the male comes from the female and, for balance, the male must always be connecting to the female in one continuous flow."

"I'm with you so far."

"Somewhere, sometime, there were those who didn't get initiated. For whatever reasons: disruptions in the normal flow of ceremonies, the reminders of the sacred; inattention, temporarily forgetting how important the initiation is, because no one's ever seen how far off course uninitiated males can go. By the time the examples were becoming obvious, it was too late. A patriarchy emerged to do battle with the ways of Goddess, to stand not with but above and over Mother Earth. New male-only or male-above-all stories were invented. The journey into the womb of Earth was rejected, forgotten and demeaned. No longer did young men have the opportunity to know her ground in that deep intimate way, immersed in soft dirt, with the same delight as pure water."

"Lovely."

"When man stands apart from woman, lording it over her, he becomes vicious, violent, brutal and cruel. The male needs the tempering of the female to prevent the solar fire energy from becoming destructive. Think of the sun by himself, pure fire that consumes everything in its path. When that solar energy is filtered through miles and miles of open air and then mates with Mother Earth in her resplendent and variegated glory, many beautiful things are born of that union. Modern science calls it photosynthesis and can show us pictures of what happens at the microcosmic level."

"The other ages of woman, when do I...?" Wu asked.

"All in due course. There's plenty of time...and no time."

"I understand that. Why am I not afraid?"
"Preparation...and you're in Her care."

S/he found herself playing with dolls and inhabiting a body that felt about ten or eleven. A gentle rain fell outside the adobe house. The dolls were made of cornhusks and scraps of old clothes. The devotion she felt for her doll pervaded her being, and just then her mother appeared and handed her a babe in arms. Her instincts heightened with the live baby. She cooed softly in his ear. "Sissy loves you; just like Mommy loves you." Her heart expanded to envelop the entire baby in an aura of warmth and safety. Aura wrapped within aura wrapped within aura all the way to the Great Mother herself, yet s/he somehow knew that "Wu" was still her name. Why was that important?

Just then her mother returned, and Wu knew that Gordon was his mother, a woman of substantial proportions. The mother sat and Wu passed the baby back to her. An aura of love in proportion to the size of her body emanated from Gordon. Mother Love pervaded the whole house. Little girl Wu was on that threshold basking in the Mother Love, while feeling herself moving toward being that Mother Love and loving and admiring her mother, all of it an appealing divine ache in her heart.

"Will we learn how a man like this boy-child can learn to be the right kind of man?" Wu asked later.

"It starts with our grounding as women. When we have truly gotten the experience of woman, of Goddess, then and only then is it safe to be a man." Gordon, still in his Great Mother body, turned to regard this fellow who asked all the right questions. "Do I look a little like Buddha?"

Wu took a long hard look. "Very little," he finally replied.

"Darn, I been trying for that."

"Is it difficult to attain?"

"Apparently." They both chuckled as Gordon began to morph into the paunchy American tourist.

"Why do you choose to walk around in that body?"

"I could ask, 'Why do you ask?', but I'll answer first. Surface level: incognito; no one suspects someone who looks like me of being up to any mystical shenanigans. I'm still looking at my prejudice toward someone who looks like me. Be honest. What was your first reaction when you met me?"

"Well, it was kind of a crisis, but I know what you're talking about. I got to know you so quickly, didn't have time to play with prejudice. I might easily have wondered, 'What's he doing here'. I'm not a good case study. I've met so many different people in my life; most stereotypes faded away long ago. What about your prejudice?"

"The last time I was born on earth I was in a Native American body; it was not a good time. This body that I walk around in is the stereotype of the white destroyer, the latest evolution of males cut off from their feminine roots. We had to dance for them while they took pictures, people who looked just like me now."

"How's this practice working for you?"

"If I'd mastered it, I wouldn't still be in this body. I need to have more compassion and understanding for myself, my current self anyway."

"Isn't it a cycle that perpetuates itself. You know. Hurt people hurt people."

"I have this place inside my belly where souls come to be born." Wu could not believe what s/he was saying, much less what s/he was feeling. "The miracle of life happens inside my body."

"You are the passageway between this world and the other

world."

"Yeah, me and every other woman."

"Let's talk culture. Imagine you're a boy growing up in ancient times," Gordon began. "All of your role-modeling, all your positive reinforcement, everything you see tells you that true men are by nature gentle souls whose highest aspiration is to be helpful and useful. On top of that there's the initiation which confers direct experience of the mystical magic of the feminine existence, her inherent connection with the infinitely fertile creativity of the spirit-that-moves-in-all-things."

"So as men we can be equally as tuned in, but we have to consciously pursue it and recognize it for what it is, a feminine fertility process which we are part of."

"One of the most important teachings or cultural patterns is about sexual roles. Women were seen as the active partners, the aggressors if you like. The coolest thing a guy can do is be really receptive."

"Am I to understand that societies of women are the most ancient, like Shee and her cohorts in the Celtic Isles before the birth of Turtle Island. How did they reproduce?"

"They were more or less immortal. If they wanted to create a new being, there was a highly focused ceremony to do that."

"Okay, I get the gender role thing. Daphne and I have practiced fully clothed tantra for several years now. And it was her idea in the beginning. How do we convert back? We been running this deadly program for many centuries."

"That's the ultimate question, isn't it? Before we get to that, have you heard the story of the Sheela-na-gig?"

"Not by that name."

"When the first church fathers arrived in Ireland, they wanted to build churches. In many places they were told they could build a church so long as they place an image over the door of a woman with her legs spread and her hands drawing attention to her genitals. That is the Sheela-na-gig. Some of those old churches are still standing. One religion emphasizes a dead god hanging on a cross as their number one symbol. The other is clearly focused on birth and the passageway between the worlds."

"So many things that were concepts, kind of like abstract painting; now I get more fully the good fortune of placing the male below the female," Wu observed.

"Yes, often when we men try to take control, we make quite a mess of things, not just in the sexual arena."

"Where else, Gordon?"

"Parenting, but let me say in modern times I'm not just talking men and women. We have women with exaggerated male traits. We have men with exaggerated female traits. The main problem started with the hijacking of the spiritual realm by a gang of male-only godheads. The loss of Goddess in everyday life is about as profound an underlying factor as anything we can point to."

"I get it that I'm still part of a largely patriarchal lineage, as much as we try to espouse and live in balance, and in modern times you find many women steeping their souls in the ancient traditions, and if they search deeply enough, they will find the elusive core essence of womanhood, of Goddess, of Earth Mother."

"I believe they are, like your friend, Daphne."

"Yes, we teach each other. I feel quite innocent in her presence."

"Taoist Mother Goddess?"

"Kwan Yin."

"So Wu, are you ready to experience sex as a woman?"

The question was sudden, but Wu had been expecting it. "I don't know. I haven't experienced sex as a man."

"You might be a special case. You made a vow of celibacy at an early age. Maybe I should start by telling you a story."

"I like that. You know, I get the whole cultural programming thing and how distorted the definitions of maleness have become, compared to the times when initiations ensured the balance of those in male bodies. But what do we do now, when things have gone so far the other direction?"

"Do you know the story I'm going to tell you? It's one answer to your question." Gordon extracted a manuscript from the bag he often carried. "This was written by a young man I worked with, who wrote it about his own experiences and gave it to me some years ago. It's one example of how we may reintroduce the ancient wisdom into the modern world. You may experience this story as an observer or a participant or whatever combination is most comfortable for you."

Initiation

We take spiritual initiation when we become
conscious of the Divine within us, and thereby
contact the Divine without us.
~ Dion Fortune

"I had just turned eighteen, so what did I know about what's real and what's not. My dad had always been a liberal, but had not revealed any woo-woo tendencies when I was growing up. So when he told me I was going on a road trip with him and my uncle, I didn't think too much of it. I kinda thought we might be doing some kind of macho adventure together, you know, four-wheeling across the high desert or climbing a mountain. And my memory of some of what happened is really sketchy. Some of what happened during those four days is crystal clear. The rest of it must be on a need to remember basis. I'm sure my mom had something to do with setting it up, but we never talked about it."

"That's ten years ago already," Darrin declared.

"Yeah, I know."

"I have the feeling you're going to tell me something really heavy. You sure I have a need to know?"

Jed chuckled. "I don't know, but I have a need to tell. You've been my best friend forever. It's something really important that happened to me. I need to start talking about it to a select few."

"Okay, my friend, fire away."

"We went somewhere out in the wilds of central Nevada. Didn't see too many people. Passed a couple of Indian reservations. Saw some antelope. We stopped by an unmarked dirt road leading farther into unknown territory. Two women eventually came to meet us. A few miles up the dirt road, they showed us where to leave our car. We proceeded as passengers in their SUV."

"What were the women like?"

"Not particularly beautiful, but not ugly. Friendly, but not very talkative. They told us to relax and enjoy the ride. Suggested if we closed our eyes, we might see some interesting things."

"Did you?"

"Yeah, and it was like I'd dropped a tab of acid, but I hadn't. Lots of swirling beautiful colors and a definite sense of starting to feel really, really good. That diminished if I opened my eyes, so I kept them closed most of the time."

"Did the women have names? How old were they?"

"They seemed a little younger than my mom. One introduced herself as Mata and the other, who hardly talked at all but gave off a friendly vibe, I was told her name and immediately forgot it. Next thing I knew we had obviously arrived at our destination. It was like an oasis in the desert, lots of greenery and flowers everywhere. The buildings blended in with the landscape. You almost had to look twice and really concentrate to see them."

"Then what?"

"I was turned over to two other women, who I would also describe as plain and middle-aged. They led me away to one of the buildings. I looked back to my dad. He just nodded and smiled and mouthed the words, 'This is your birthday present.' I decided to relax and go along for the ride, whatever it was."

"I'm already hooked."

"The building housed a large hot tub spa, several beds and soft, comfortable furniture. They invited me to sit."

Jed told the story to the best of his recollection.

Jasmine began. "Do you know why you're here?"

"No, not exactly."

"Okay sweetheart, this is orientation 1A."

Jed felt totally cool with her calling him sweetheart. In fact he liked it and felt more and more drawn to her as she talked. He was looking right at her as she changed. Her age, body type, ethnicity, everything about her just kept changing as Jed listened to her tell him why he was there.

"Your father and your uncle are initiates. Your mother, as you know, is part of a group known as the Goddess Circle. This place, where you are right now, is one of our Goddess Sanctuaries, where we are free to practice the old ways of peace and sacred pleasure that have virtually disappeared in these recent centuries of patriarchy. What you will experience is similar to what all young men went through in the ancient times of Goddess. The role of sexuality in these modern times is very distorted. The promise that humans had to pleasure themselves into peace and well-being has become extremely diluted. If it happens at all, it doesn't last, and life goes back to the competition and violence which is so pervasive in the modern age."

"You said initiation. Is this some ordeal that I'm about to experience?"

"Quite the opposite, this is an initiation into pleasure, to understand pleasure as an integral part of the sacred, to understand the way that pleasure connects humans with each other, an essential bond in families and communities."

"Sounds good to me."

"Okay, if you're ready to proceed, I'll give you a few minutes. You can remove your clothes and leave them on the couch. Just kick back in the spa and I'll join you shortly."

When she came back, another woman accompanied her. Jed was in awe. They were the most beautiful women he'd ever seen in his life. He would have done anything they asked of him. Their requests were simple.

"Just relax and let us do everything. It's like you're getting the best massage you've ever had. This is Calypso. We'll both be touching you all over your body. Is that all right?"

"Absolutely, I'm putty in your hands."

"We hope so. So just lay back and float on your back. We'll support you so you don't sink. Do you trust us?"

"Implicitly."

"Excellent, we trust you too. There is no intention of harm or unfair advantage by any of us. Close your eyes and allow yourself an inward journey. We'll be silent except for the celestial music you hear, but if you need something or something comes up for you it's okay to speak up. Sometimes we tag-team, so if you feel different hands, don't worry. That's why."

Jed lay back, floating on his back. He felt four hands, both delicate and strong, holding and supporting him. Floating seemed easy. Maybe there was something in the water. Soon all thoughts drifted away. All awareness was focused on the loving hands that made him feel like the most loved infant. He heard the sounds that a loving mother makes. Were the women cooing to him, or was it his imagination? It didn't matter. He coasted on the rhythms of pleasure their touch elicited in his body and in his being. "Never felt this good before." One thought that quickly dissolved into the shapes and colors of orchids and lilies and abstract patterns that might have been swirling rainbows, the deep throats of flowers or the entrance to a holy woman.

He felt himself passing through the birth canal back into a womb of such delicious comfort, tactile sensations he couldn't remember until he was experiencing them again. Totally held and protected, floating in a universe, slick and soft and tasty. Yes, there was a taste. "Must be ambrosia," he thought.

"We are going to teach you how to make love with a woman by loving you the way we like to be loved." Jasmine spoke softly. It felt to Jed like her words were rolled in honey and slid across a liquid universe directly into his brain where they further dissolved and penetrated every neuron with a delicious sweetness. He felt so trusting of them. He was an infant with two loving and totally devoted mothers, whom he had no reason not to totally surrender to.

Their touching gradually moved to the more intimate parts of his body. They massaged and pinched and licked and sucked his nipples. He was surprised at how sensitive he was. Their fingers and mouths generated waves of pleasure throughout his body. He felt an intense love for both of them. He was steeped in their love for him. He wanted to touch them but knew that he didn't get to do that yet. They rubbed and massaged his hands and placed them on their own breasts as they continued to knead and squeeze and milk his fingers. Their breasts became ethereal clouds and at the same time perfectly squishy but firm water balloons.

At first they ignored his erection, but eventually stroked all around his responsiveness, reaching between his legs, squeezing his butt cheeks and very lightly stroking the length of his shaft before moving away again. He moaned and gasped, twisting beneath their touch. Inevitably his body responded and white cum spewed from him. They continued to stroke and squeeze as he expelled the pleasure he could no longer contain. Each kept a hand on his shrinking staff as they kissed his face and lips; tongue on tongue they explored his mouth slipping and sliding along his interior membranes. He'd never felt anything like that and began to get turned on again. His phallus, which they had taken ownership of, was already filling up and rising.

They took turns kissing and exploring his lips and tongue, or licked and nipped each other's lips and tongue along the way. Their desire for each other fueled their desire for him. It was so wonderful to be wanted like that. One of them continued kissing him and stroking his face and head and pinching his nipples. Calypso slowly moved down his body and took control of his full erection. She licked and stroked; she took his entire length in her mouth and throat. She was driving him wild. He had to come up for air with Jasmine. She dangled a breast in front of his mouth, so he could lick and suck when he had the breath to engage. He was losing focus among the delights they were serving him. Calypso's delicate fingers were sometimes barely there, and then she would grasp him strongly and release again. "This must be heaven," he thought before succumbing again and again to the waves of pleasure that now seemed to radiate from Calypso's fingers.

He wanted to give back and so latched onto Jasmine's perfectly round and full breast. When he became too vigorous, she backed away, holding and massaging both his cheeks as she proffered her bounty once again. Gradually he got the hang of slow and gentle until she began to moan as well. "Hum," she suggested, and he did, sending new shivers and tingles through her nipple and then her whole body. There was an expanding warmth between her legs and into her lower belly. Ordinarily she might pull away and slow things down, but she was fascinated by her own body's response. "Could I orgasm just from his licking and sucking my breast?"

So she did not move away. Occasionally she glanced toward Calypso to admire the meticulous care she was applying to the young man's phallus, treating it like it was the most beautiful, deserving-of-love object in the world. Kissing, stroking, squeezing, rubbing, but all with a delicacy that felt like a tease but was also working a magic that had Jed on the edge of orgasm again. Then she backed away except for the hand that firmly held his balls. He got it that the best thing for him to do was keep his focus on loving the breast that had been given to him. What intensity he felt as he began to dance with Jasmine, to sense her responses to him, to respond to her responses, to notice the effects of his care for her. He was drawn to do whatever she wanted, to pleasure her as he was being pleasured.

Then Calypso came to his other side, took his hand in her own and guided it to her lovely soft breast. With her hand over his, he was rubbing and squeezing her breast. She was showing him exactly how to touch her. Her elegant fingers were teaching his fingers the nuances of loving a woman's breast. Meanwhile Jasmine moved between his legs like a hummingbird discovering a rare flower with her long tongue. Lightly she licked hither and thither. Where would he feel her tongue tip next? Where would the blade tease him into greater fullness? How could something so small feel like the most loving caress. She licked him like he was the most delicious ice cream, like she could hardly wait for the next taste. She alternately cupped and squeezed his cheeks with her full hands or toyed with his balls and their sac and circled the base of his cock while rimming the head with her hummingbird tongue.

Calypso had released his hand so that now he roamed freely over both breasts, totally tuned into what she responded to and going more and more for that repertoire. She was very turned on and let him know. "Oh yes, that, more of that," so he was getting verbal as well as sensory feedback. Calypso could have jumped on him right then, but she knew how to prolong, how to savor, how to build ever so slowly to a stupendous climax. Succumbing to orgasm could feel like abandoning some creative process that was so engrossing, so all-encompassing. This young man was such a quick study: "Very tuned in; I like that," she reflected.

Gradually Jasmine applied more and more pressure. She looked up and caught Calypso's eye. Their love for each other just flowed easily and naturally. Was she asking, "Who wants to take him?" but Calypso was already back with the sensation radiating from the loving hands on her breasts. Jasmine brought him to the edge numerous times and backed off to forestall the inevitable climax. Finally she could feel the prophetic spasms; they had passed the point of no return. She took him into her mouth, held him there and lightly sucked as he spasmed again and again. She swallowed everything and let him rest in her mouth awhile. As he slowly shrank, she massaged him with her lips and tongue sending more spasms through his body. She dallied over his intimate parts, making them familiar enough to be her own. He felt profoundly honored and accepted by these two beautiful women, these Goddesses or priestesses of Goddess.

The next day Jed was again welcomed by the two women to join them in the spa. They both wore silk robes that tied at the waist. He wore only the loose drawstring trousers they had provided for him. Others had brought him a delicious breakfast of fresh fruit, homemade sausage and toast. He felt fit and excited for what the day might bring to him.

At the spa the two women cast aside their robes, entered the water and extended their arms to invite him in. He shed his pants and willingly joined them. For a while they soaked in the warmth of the pool. Then Jasmine laid on one of the cushions that surrounded the spa, her legs dangling in the water. Then she rested her feet on two ledges that lay just below the water. Far enough apart that her knees were raised and her legs comfortably spread to reveal a lovely vulva, the petals pink and slightly swollen from the warmth. He and Calypso could comfortably move between Jasmine's legs. Already it seemed like a perfect day to him. Calypso spoke for the first time. "I am going to show you what to do. Just do as I do. Remember there is no goal. Just make love slowly, sincerely and deliciously."

Calypso laid one hand on Jasmine's belly. Jasmine covered it with her own hand and squeezed slightly as if signaling to proceed. With her other hand Calypso delicately spread her girlfriend's nether lips. Jasmine's vulva was a blooming flower. Calypso licked all around Jasmine's golden peach. At the first touch of tongue to lips there was a sharp catch of breath and then soft moans. Calypso continued her slow savoring of this delicious fruit before approaching the swollen knob of her clitoris. As her tongue probed the symmetry of her hood and slid blithely over the engorgement it shrouded, there were more moans and sharp gasps when a particularly sensitive spot was grazed.

Then Calypso stepped back and motioned for Jed to continue what she had begun. He was immediately intoxicated by the taste and smell of Jasmine's pink lady-slipper. He imitated what he had seen Calypso do and was pleased with what he heard from Jasmine, who was sucking on Calypso's fingers. He dared to press his stiff tongue inside her orifice, which elicited a louder moan. He slowly slid in and out between her inner lips and slick canal. Calypso stroked his head to give further encouragement. Jed again felt honored by the approval of both women. It was like a preschooler hearing, "Good job," and basking in the glow of such appreciation.

As Jasmine's passion continued to grow, Calypso gently pulled Jed away from his delightful duties and interposed herself. She kissed Jed full on the mouth sliding her tongue in and out in a way that made Jed hunger for more. Her hand momentarily slid along his erection. Then she held up one finger and moved again to Jasmine's holy aperture. "G-spot," she declared softly and slid her finger into the slick folds of supple flesh. Jed watched closely to see as much as he could exactly what she was doing. "The lightest touch," she murmured.

When it was Jed's turn, Jasmine grasped his hand and moved it so that his finger was in the right place. "Just move a little. Slip and slide." Again she showed him by moving his hand with hers. He quickly got the hang of it.

"Improvise," Calypso whispered, as she rubbed her fingers over the monk's hood and then stuck them in Jed's mouth. He hummed appreciatively, withdrew his fingers and slid them in

Calypso's mouth. They both sucked until the taste was gone. Then Jed leaned into Jasmine once more, probing her with his tongue, trying to reach her G-spot, sliding his tongue around her hooded lady and then penetrating again.

"That feels so good," Jasmine exclaimed. Calypso was sucking and licking her nipples, and then she moved to kiss her: deep, long and slow. Her extension to meet the other mouth exposed her perfectly round butt. Jed reached with one hand to knead and massage and lightly slide a finger between her cheeks. She gasped and ground lips against the lips of the other woman. Jed continued to slide into the slippery wetness of her pink canoe. He was careful to be slow and gentle with both women, and they were responding as if he was the best lover ever, some incarnation of Pan.

Calypso crawled out of the pool and lowered herself on Jasmine's face. Jasmine accommodated by kissing and licking the petals of her tasty cave: lip to lip, active tongue, as if they were French kissing mouth to mouth. Jed could see their action from his vantage point where he was lavishing his most loving labial caresses on Jasmine's yawning lulu-belle. When Calypso drew him to another cushion and laid him on his back, he did not resist. She immediately lowered herself to his kisser, and he was ready for her. Meanwhile Jasmine rolled over and guided his hand to her slick deep dish and sat on his upraised finger. "Don't move," she commanded. The subtle rolling of her hips provided all the stimulation she required until she replaced his finger with his now throbbing erection.

So slowly she lowered herself onto his expectant member. She accomplished the same slow roll she'd been plying on his other appendage. He continued to acquiesce to the exquisite leisurely rhythm of both women, open-mouthed he was and standing at attention. They took their time and leaned in to kiss each other. All of their affection for the other poured forth, holding tongues between lips sliding in and out of each other's welcoming mouths. Hands entwined in magnificent manes and stroking smooth faces, while continuing a delicate rhythm of ballroom dance on the willing partner who couldn't believe his fortune to have two beauties gifting him their most intimate parts. He felt heroic, blessed and honored by their loving kindness. He felt further exalted to be in the aura of their profound love so deliciously expressed for each other. He felt chosen by two Goddesses who were absolutely lovely in every way.

The subdued movement kept him intensely stimulated and emotionally excited while sufficiently distant from any climactic edge. Effortlessly he got to be their baby, their divine child. When they switched positions, he was in such bliss he hardly noticed except that though Calypso was the more voluptuous of the two, she was tighter inside. Jasmine's labia were fuller and more swollen and, in that sense, more intriguing to slide his lips and tongue on and in, as if there were some mystery he was searching for but would never find. The women seemed tireless in their expression of loving desire for each other. He basked in the ecstasy of it all, dimly aware that he was experiencing a gift that few were so divined to receive.

In the middle of it all they rolled off him and lay on their backs. "Make love to us," Calypso murmured. "Keep it slow, so you can maintain. Let the pleasure build little by little."

Jasmine added, "We love you. We love your attention. There is no hurry. There is no goal. Just be with us and love us."

"We have all the time in the world."

Jed sat between his two ravishing beauties. "Les belles," he declared softly, while gently placing a hand on each mound of Venus he had already had such an intimate connection with. His erection was almost unbearable, but he was determined to be a good student, to learn by explicitly following their instructions. From his position he first leaned into Calypso. He was so attracted to her breasts. He kissed and licked them as if they were the most sacred objects he'd ever touched. He slid two fingers into the throat of her flower, circling around that most sensitive area he'd been introduced to. Calypso let out a deep sign and squirmed beneath his touch. Suckling at her breast, he felt like her best baby and her best lover at the same time.

As he was getting lost in Calypso, Jasmine extended a sly hand between his legs and began to dandle and squeeze his balls like they were her favorite toy. The action pulled some of the intensity from his erection and spread it around his whole pelvic area. "One way to last longer," he thought.

"Come inside me," Calypso groaned. As he shifted positions to enter her, she continued. "Very slowly, slide your length in and out." And then, "That's it, just like that." Jasmine repositioned herself just above Calypso's face, so Calypso could lick and kiss but had room to breathe if she needed. This slick slow rhythm was bringing Calypso along rather quickly. She grabbed Jasmine's hips to focus all her passion into her girlfriend's delicious flower, grinding her lips into the other woman's lips, licking and poking with her tongue, grasping any protuberance with her own lips. Then she grabbed Jed's butt to pull him into her as far as she could. All three of them could feel an impending orgasm, a fireworks finale to all their meticulous melodies and highlife harmonies.

When she felt him beginning to cum, Calypso clutched him as tight and close as she could, wanting to get all of him, while Jasmine ground and twisted her hip-hop fantasia and loudly announced the thunder that was coming over her. Jed also cut loose louder than he ever had. Together they raised a holy cacophony that shook the high desert air and accompanied the eruptions of their bodies and the communion of their spirits.

The next day was another lesson. In the meantime, Jed was well fed and well rested, anticipating the arrival of his Goddess teachers. He wore only his drawstring pants when they arrived in their loose-fitting robes. He willingly accompanied them to the spa area, where they directed him to sit cross-legged on one of the cushions. Calypso began. "I want you to look into my eyes. Keep your gaze there no matter what else I do." Her one hand trailed down to his glorious tumescence. She toyed with him lightly while holding his gaze, watching his eyes melt, watching their eyes melt into each other. She kissed him briefly, then continued the steady warm ogling. His eyes spoke the warmth that was rising in him. He loved these women. How could he not? They had treated him like the most cherished prince, the hero son of Goddess. Love and gratitude gushed from him in response.

When Calypso kissed him more earnestly, he responded in kind. Her slender fingers found his smooth cheeks and combed through his hair. He felt Jasmine's fingers on his jade stalk and then her tongue licked its length and then she totally enclosed him in her soft mouth. She sucked her cheeks in to hold him more firmly and relaxed them again. He could not describe the exotic ecstasy as his purple warrior of love was trapped in her lacuna and was released again. He squirmed underneath her while trying his best to maintain his deep kissing with Calypso, who swung a leg around his torso poised just above Jasmine, who released the purple warrior, casually licked Calypso's protruding vulva and guided her recent captive into an expectant sheath.

With a hand on the lower back of her conjoined lovers, she crooned, "Just be very quiet for awhile. Notice every sensation." Her hands stroked two dorsa; she hummed and murmured sweet nothings near two ears: "My lover, my sweet, my favorite dessert, feel the love of Goddess coming from me, from each other, from all of Her." Then she hummed and trilled an ethereal melody of love everlasting and beyond the beyond. She was an angel from the realm of Venus singing sweet songs like never before.

"This day will never be bygone," she warbled as from somewhere inside both of them.

They sat obediently and savored waves and undulations of bliss and beatitudes. If yesterday had been earthly love, today was heavenly love, coasting on a cloud of euphoria, sly sloop in a gentle breeze, trade winds of a summer sea. Love poured from every chakra, expansive, inclusive, growing the circle, loving Jasmine and loving everyone who occurred to them.

Things slowed down even more. Jasmine's hands stopped moving and rested on their low backs. With absolutely no movement, Jed maintained a full erection. He could feel a throbbing from the flesh of Calypso's jade gate. Occasionally he felt waves of warmth that seemed to start and end in arbitrary places. She could feel those waves; they were inside her. Without any movement she felt an acute presence, a personal cantilever that reached up inside of her seeking to touch her core essence. She yearned for that touch. If only her soul could be caressed, deeply and sincerely. They were in these moments Goddess and God, Shiva and Shakti, Chandra and Tara, Ulysses and Calypso, and other divine couples. They all sat together like this in perfect contemplation of their own core essence and each other's. It's all the same at that most essential level of the many layered chocolate tree. Yes, they were lapsing into poetry together in that idyllic bubble of just enough desire to maintain a certain level of elation.

Imagining themselves in other lifetimes symbiotically conjoined Goddess and God, cloud drifting over a peaceful ocean, southern trade winds riding a turtle from essence to essence, one fragrance after another, gardens of lily ponds and arched bridges.

In another lifetime they poured over that special manuscript, marathons of days and nights to ensure that just the right word had been put in just the right context. What a dialogue, two monks of some ancient sect wandering mountains in the warmth of their own beliefs and practices. An ancient sect from the beginning of time on earth, they continued to practice the simple, comfortable path they knew, no matter what changes some modern world tried to impose. Long hair streaming in the wind that blew through every cell and pore, enlivening and enlightening by its very essence of freedom, blowing through everything.

In the shade of a beaver lodge the lazy big cat prowls, all held within the mind and arms and heart of a greater being. In this biological world we are all eating one another. We can also pose or dance with the balance of fire to hold us in our dreams. We are gone, gone beyond, gone beyond the beyond, beyond those highest mountains in a hidden valley that no one can find without invitation, the Original Ones still live, the Creator's firstborn on Earth. Whenever we sit as we are now, we are with them riding one beam of their radiance, beings of almost pure Spirit. We and they are one right now.

It was so much to feel, yet not overwhelming at all, an easy float trip down a quiet river, wild goats and glacial melt on a summer's day. A telepathic conversation ensued. "Can I come here again?"

"Anytime."

"Do I need a partner?"

"Not always in the flesh."

"You would visit me in spirit."

"Of course, my darling, and so would many others, who sit as we are sitting now."

"It feels like utter selflessness."

The fourth day was conversation and frivolity. "So what have you learned, young Jed?" Jasmine asked. "Your final reward will come later."

Jed sat in an armless chair munching on toast and fruit and sipping fresh-brewed coffee. He felt like the luckiest guy in the world. These women had to be some gift from Goddess. He hoped he'd continue to be worthy of them. His answer came haltingly as if he was just putting it together in the moment. "Go slow; follow her lead; tune in; be responsive. Let her make love to you!" he giggled. "Give, make love to her. Be her other half, tuned in, morphing to complement her shapes as she continually changes in response to the wonder of the moment."

That last one caused Calypso and Jasmine to grin and look meaningfully at one another. "You've been paying attention, and you're a poet. Wow!"

"So what happens today?"

"You're just rarin' to go, aren't you?"

He grinned at Jasmine. "Only when you are."

"Quick learner too."

Soon the women retired to the spa, floating and propelling themselves from one side to the other.

"May I join you," he asked.

"Certainly," they retorted in unison with a sing-song trill in their voices.

Soon he was soaking and floating. The women gravitated to him. Jasmine toyed with his breakfast link. Maybe she'd turn it into a banger. Calypso massaged his butt cheeks and slid her finger back and forth between them. Jed almost shivered despite the warm water.

"Soon we will go to the cushions. Today is your day to initiate, to direct if you will. Remember everything you have learned about how to please us. Assume you're with a woman of little experience, and you have to educate her. Good turns of phrase are like, 'Can I show you something'. Invite her to do something she hasn't done before. At first, choose one of us, like this was an average date. You will remember everything we've taught you." The last part was encouragement, not command.

The women retired to the close-at-hand cushions. They sat

cross-legged and smiled to themselves, looking casual and demure in their clean nudity. Jed decided to approach Calypso. He had really bonded with her yesterday during the tantra session. He sat cross-legged in front of her. "Hi, my name's Jed."

"Calypso."

"I'd like to hang out with you, Calypso."

"That would be cool."

After a few more pleasantries, Jed asked, "Would you like a massage?"

"I'd love one." She lay on her stomach and waited. Jed straddled her and began to work her back and shoulders. Jasmine handed him some massage oil. He took his time, long strokes along either side of her backbone, kneading the muscles of her shoulder and neck. He really took his time, gradually sliding beside her to better access her butt and legs which were more muscular than he had remembered. Occasionally Calypso moaned softly as she breathed ever deeper. She murmured, "Lovely," or "Right there."

Jed was erect now. He dragged his pleasure wand between her legs and cheeks, liberally dashed with lavender massage oil. She loved his hard flesh on her inner thighs.

"You can turn over now if you'd like."

When she did, he exclaimed, "Your body is stunningly beautiful." His hands sought the supple flesh of her round bosom. "Like a water balloon, only firmer," he thought. Unable to resist any longer his mouth went to one nipple: licking, pressing, sucking, while the other continued tender treatment from his free hand. Calypso began to moan and squirm as he focused on her upper body, kissing and licking her belly, hands roaming everywhere, exploring, stroking, seeking new and old points of pleasure. He trailed his fingers through her dark muff, loving the texture of this nether hair. His fingers found her ultra-smooth lips but did not linger there, moving instead to stroke her inner thighs and squeeze her calves.

Her legs were opening to all his touches. He leaned in and

licked her vulva once and then again focused on everything else, sucking and tonguing her ripe areolas and the stamens that projected from her twin flowers. She seemed darker than ever today, which all the more drew him to her. Finally he gave in and brought his head beneath her thighs, at first just casually licking, probing a little, flesh playing with flesh. For a while he settled into probing with his tongue, then withdrawing. He curled his tongue up to tantalize her matrix before sliding out. And then he was there again. Calypso could not remember anyone doing this with her. She held his head to draw him closer when he entered. Her lava was already flowing over the top and down the sides, red-hot licorice that did not burn, tempered by ice-blue mint that did not freeze. Can't get enough, or this is just right; just keep it going.

Jed could tell that he had stumbled into something quite wonderful. He could feel it. He stayed with his probing, extending his tongue as far as he could until Calypso spilled over in every direction clutching his head to her matrix of pleasure, slowly sliding down from her peak of pleasure; finally she shuddered no more. She let go of everything and lay spent. Jed kissed her one last time before turning to Jasmine, the lither and lighter of the two. He motioned for her to join him. Soon they were sitting as Goddess and God, the way he had done with Calypso the day before. The feeling was more ethereal than with Calypso, a difference in sensations that was hard to describe but equally delightful. When they joined, when he slid inside her, a wave of warm love passed over and through both of them. In unison they gasped, "I love you."

That was the experience. In this divine meditative posture there was instant pure love that both involved and didn't involve their bodies. They easily moved into the still silence together and thus communed for several hours while Calypso lay sleeping beside them.

They journeyed together to that valley hidden in the highest mountains on Earth, the place that is never seen, the place where the cloud bodies of the sages hang suspended above the highest peaks, contemplating from time immemorial and incorporeal how it is all playing out at all the lower elevations, the fires scorching earth and Mother Kali Ocean pregnantly bursting her waters to quench them. A strange, almost random thought occurred to him. "Fear-mongers, violent and hateful ones, is this the best we can do to combat them?"

"We will outlast them always." The silent voice of the sages resonated through icy blue chimes.

"Such peace! Such Joy! What else can we possibly need?"

They had left their bodies and traveled to the place of Her first children, the infinite portal where all of us are still connected with those Ancient Ones, our ancestors who walked this earth in peace and joy for thousands of years, long before they imagined a need to till the earth. In their robes and sandals they shape-shifted their perambulations, mostly at play in the fields of Grand Lady Goddess.

Manna, ambrosia, nectar falling from the sky, pouring out of the earth, they bathed in a warm ocean beside a holy candle, the eternal flame, while lying within the arms of their cloud bodies, an eternal embrace.

"It is our time in eternity."

Indeed it felt timeless and eternal as they sat conjoined and in communion with each other and with those great beings whose place on earth was the highest mountains of Asia. Feeling fervently connected with ancient wisdom, with the Spirit that moves in all things, Jed was only mildly surprised that his journey with these two women had taken a decidedly spiritual turn. From the beginning of these days at the sanctuary, he felt safe in a way that people feel in church. They had introduced themselves as priestesses. They had treated him with the utmost care, which drew him to reciprocate, to love them as tenderly as he possibly could. To now be shown a connection to an ancient spiritual tradition, perhaps *the* ancient spiritual tradition of earth, was only mildly surprising. To be shown not only the possibility, but the ancient reality that sexual relations could be entirely integrated with spiritual purpose, that was a delightful revelation.

The trance that he and Jasmine inhabited together would come to an end. He would willingly remain there forever, but understood the truth of the sages; the transmigration of souls would eventually bring him to live with the cloud beings of Shambhala, but there were many experiences and many lifetimes leading to that eventual victory. His hope for now was to never forget the strength of interconnection that he was currently experiencing in the tapestry of his deepest Self.

"Yes, we will come to you when you call us in your meditation. It will be just as it has been here. You will feel us with all your senses and regenerate the communion we have discovered and maintained with each other here. Know that we love you in a very personal way. We are your personal Sisters of Love. We are the sexy angels you have known since before you were born in this life. Love at this level is infinite because it is synchronized with that infinite wellspring of love you have danced with in these last days."

Calypso continued where Jasmine left off. "There is no jealousy. There is no fear. We are mellifluous, harmonic, celestial spheres mutually stimulating the liveliness and the tranquility of the divine."

What Comes Natural

Being natural is incredibly
empowering for women
because it's just who you are.
~ Rozonda Thomas

In the warmth of an afternoon Daphne fell asleep in the back seat of the jeep, and she dreamed a dream that seemed to go on forever. She had been a close companion with Wu for several years, but had never felt a romantic or sexual attraction toward him.

In the dream at first nothing was particularly different than it ever had been. They sat together in tantric practice, fully clothed as they always had been. She felt relaxed and comfortable, resting on familiar ground. Then, almost imperceptibly they were no longer clothed, and he was inside of her. What was remarkable was that this felt totally unremarkable, like "no big deal", like something they had done many times before. The sense in the dream was that they sat in this way for several hours, the periodic waves of sexual energy were easily incorporated into their mutual meditation and augmented their practice of cultivating spiritual awareness.

"Easy, pleasant, natural" were the words she would have used to describe this unprecedented experience of feeling such personal love for Wu. "I wonder if this will ever happen," she mused several times, when she wasn't so immersed that she felt like it was actually happening. She knew she did not want to leave the place she was in. She knew that she and Wu were more powerfully joined than ever before, for them the next step in their evolution together, as they each prepared for their roles in what lay ahead in the planetary transition. As the scene began to slowly fade away, a solitary voice, seemingly from far away, simply recited, "So many paths to explore." It might have been her voice.

When she finally awoke from the dream, it was a slow gradual process of coming into consciousness. The dream was still vividly with her. She wouldn't forget this one. The experience was not all that different from the monks' tantra they'd been practicing for a while. Yet it was different. She'd never had feelings of romantic love for a man. It definitely felt more personal than it had been throughout their relationship. She'd never considered the possibility that she was bisexual. She was attracted to women, end of story. And the last two years traveling with Wu, they had both been celibate. They had never been naked with each other as they were in the dream.

"How odd," she thought, "that such a dream would come up now, when there's no chance to act on it. Time to reflect...wonder how he's doing. Wonder what he's doing. Wonder if I'm in his dreams. Now I'm really tripping? But why now? Is this part of our training or preparation? 'To know that you can be anything and everything. It's all part of my creation'. Is that what she said? Yeah, 'you will own what you haven't owned before from the whole spectrum of human experience.' I hear Grandmother often these days, conversations I thought I'd forgotten."

"I think it's important to go to Chaco Canyon." Aiyana broke into Daphne's thoughts.

Daphne switched gears smoothly. "Have you been?"

"Once when I was small. I just remember how it felt."

"And how was that?"

"Magical...and old."

"Are we near?"

"Tomorrow sometime." Atsa spoke up.

"What can you tell me about it?"

"Lots of people lived there for a long time. There's evidence that they were in contact with some type of being who lived off the earth or in another dimension," Atsa replied.

"Sounds like a vortex or a portal, doesn't it?"

"I think," Aiyana said, "that people have often been drawn to areas where the boundary with the other world is not so dense, or sometimes such areas are set aside to be available to all peoples, like sanctuaries, where there would be peace to pursue spiritual activities. The area around Sedona, Arizona, is one such place. You get out among the red rock formations. Just walk around in that country. You can feel it."

"Yeah, there's a lot of power spots around there," Atsa added. "People been going there for medicine for a long time."

"It seems," Daphne declared, "that we haven't had much of a challenge finding places to commune with the other world, enclaves in other dimensions hidden away in these remote desert mountains."

"It's time. They are showing themselves more and more. It's still dangerous, but there's also protection."

"What about guilt?" Wu asked.

"What do you mean? Can you be more specific?"

"Why do I still feel guilty sometimes, like all of this learning and practice, and I still don't measure up."

Gordon rested his chin on his hands and stared into the distance. "We all feel guilty for being less than perfect. We make mistakes, and the worst part is if you're empathic, you feel the other person's pain. You feel like **you've** caused it."

"Sounds about right, but what to do? I hate the feeling, no, I hate the physiological reactions that I have."

"You have panic attacks?"

"I guess I do."

"And you're not supposed to."

"Right."

"And what sets them off?"

"Sometimes random things like saying the wrong thing to someone or saying it in the wrong way."

"You don't talk very much. Is that why? Like fear of doing harm?"

"Yeah, frankly overwhelmed by other people's emotions until I met my teacher. I felt under his protection for a long time even after our paths separated us."

"Do you know where he is?"

"He was a wanderer too."

"Did he ever have panic attacks."

"One time he was obviously distraught and emotional. I didn't feel it was my place to intervene right then. I did ask the next day."

"What did he say?"

"He said, 'It is right of you to ask. Unfortunately I still can't talk about it.' We never spoke of it again, and there was never another incident, at least not one I was privy to."

"Would you like to know where he is?"

"That's possible?"

"I could look."

"Can I sit with that?"

"Sure."

Wu closed his eyes where he sat and was silent quite a while. Gordon wandered nearby in a kind of walking meditation focusing on the plants and rocks and scat. Then he focused on a distant mountain while holding a standing meditation in concert with his young friend, Wu.

"Many pleasant memories." Wu commented on their reverie. "I would like to see him again, if that's possible."

Gordon continued to gaze at the far-off mountain. "Would

you like to see him here or where he is?"

"I think that should be his choice."

"Okay."

"What happens now?"

"It's kinda like sending a message, but it's also a projection of myself. He knows me. We of the Sisterhood mostly know each other."

"Wait a minute. You know my teacher?"

"Yeah, we're old friends."

"Well, shut my mouth." Wu dropped into a hillbilly drawl to make his point. He'd been exposed to pretty much every-thing in SoCal.

"Come closer to me; we'll send him a picture. You know, arms around each other's shoulders, very touristy." They both gazed at the mountain for maybe five minutes. "That should do it. We were in his dream just beaming away like brothers on holiday."

They walked together. "You said, 'Sisterhood', Gordon."

"By Jove, I believe you're correct, my lad."

"Tell me more."

"The Sisterhood always was and always will be. When the grand current that runs through all things began to play with anything close to gender. Well, the grand current by our standards is an extremely feminine energy, far-flung, frivo-lous creativity flowing for new vistas without any particular effort.

"So the first beings were similar extensions of the grand current that still flows through everything. Will-o'-the-wisps, sylphs, air fairies, insubstantial yet eternal on gossamer wings and bamboo winds. Dance was the universal language. Joy was the message. For eons and eons that was enough. Sisters of the same mother, infinite time, space and the wisdom which has no words."

"This was long before the Garden and all those later sto-ries after the strife had begun."

"How did the strife begin?"

"That is the great controversy. In the later stories someone is always blaming someone else. So many elements have gotten way out of control, and it's been going on so long. Even though it's only a few thousand years, it's almost all of written history. It was all written down long after the strife had begun."

"So no one knows?"

"I wouldn't say no one. I would say it's not common knowledge. I don't know. I assume if we need to know it will be revealed at the right time."

"Who makes these decisions?"

"Ultimately our Great Mother. She has many extensions who emanate Her Oneness."

"What about those who don't recognize her?"

"It's a slow process to slowly flood the universe with a conscious awareness of her Oneness, and then how that is supposed to translate into our daily activities. And things are so precariously out of balance. But she loves all her children and wants what's best, wants each and every one of them to have what they need to pursue their heart's desire."

"To Oneness."

"To Oneness."

Each of them knelt on the earth and raised their hands to the sky. Wu was inspired to put his forehead on Earth Mother and extend his hands behind him, palms facing the sky.

"I've had some strange thoughts about original sin." Wu began their next conversation.

Gordon looked at him quizzically. "Please enlighten me."

"Well, first of all it has nothing to do with Adam and Eve or any of the other derivative stories designed by the patriarchy to justify their existence and abuse of power."

"Good start."

"Contemplating my own relationship with guilt and shame, it's come up often enough in my meditations, and it always seems to go back to hazy memories that are simply stored as awful feelings of guilt and shame. The clearer, later memories are my parents shaming me for some minor infraction. The emotional pain is almost unbearable."

He paused for a while. Finally Gordon asked, "And original sin?"

"That's it. Original sin is the guilt and shame our parents lay on us before we even understand what's happening. We're left with a hazy but intense sense of having done something wrong even though we can't remember exactly what it is. Then patriarchal institutions like the Catholic Church come along and make it all cosmic, like it's some kind of negative birthright that all human beings share because of Adam's disobedience of God, the Father."

"What's the advantage to them?"

"It's a super control trip. First they poison you by instilling all this guilt, and then your only way of getting rid of this guilt is by following their guidelines to the letter, the confessional, reciting the rosary, parroting back the catechism. We have to do all this because our ancient ancestor was a disobedient child to his father."

"Does their system work?"

"In what sense?"

"Does it rid a person of the guilt and shame, the original sin?"

Wu had to think about that for a while. "It works in the way any sincere spiritual discipline works. Meditation, for instance, is an affirmation of the Oneness through a very simple practice. When one is totally in the flow of one's breathing, it is all the air and space in the universe. Doing something on a daily basis, even several times a day makes that an organizing principle in your life."

"An organizing principle, I like that."

"Like mantra, the repetition of a simple word or phrase:

Om Mani Padme Hum, the Jewel is in the Lotus, beautiful imagery for, 'The Truth is within you'. But we were talking about 'original sin' and escape from original sin."

"Yes, we were."

"Whether we see it as a common consequence of certain parental tactics or our ancient ancestor's disobedience to God, the Father. Think about the rosary, a prayer but also a mantra. It's long but the sheer precise repetition makes it mantra-like and somewhat mesmerizing."

"Okay, so far so good." Gordon grinned.

"There are certain key phrases: 'Mother of God, pray for us sinners now and at the hour of our death.' Wow, that covers it. Our Holy Mother will pray for our relief from guilt and shame of being sinners, but simultaneously relieves us of our fear of death. It's an affirmation that we can be saved from our own karma in the form of shame and guilt. How? By affirming our immersion in the Holy Mother Oneness."

"'Forgive us our trespasses as we forgive those who trespass against us, but deliver us from evil.' Powerful stuff. You've really studied this stuff."

"My teacher said it is important to investigate all serious human aspirations to wisdom and what's called holiness."

"Not your stereotypic Taoist, whatever that is."

"We defy stereotypes."

"When I first met you, you seemed so quiet and peaceful."

"All part of the flow. Daphne and I are wandering teachers. You inspire words to flow from me, philosophy, love of wisdom."

"It feels very back and forth between us, a two-way flow. Are you ready for another shape-shifting experience? I know that was a sudden shift of direction."

"Ready when you are."

"Okay, let's talk about this. You've been celibate all of this life."

"Yes."

"Why?"

"My teacher said the modern world is too obsessed with sex to the exclusion of subtler ways of associating. The mingling of energies is an ancient phenomenon when we were less tied to our physical bodies."

"Certainly, so instead of sex being virtually the only way that there is a profound mingling of energies, in ancient times it was one of many ways and of course very obviously connected with the possibility of pregnancy."

"Precisely."

"So in this next episode we're putting together, Wu, you'll be an older girl, pubescent and falling in love at the drop of a feather. You are living in a culture where that is understood and accepted. Girls live in sisterhoods where they are free to indulge all those feelings with each other."

"Because the first love was love between women, because there weren't any men yet."

"You've been paying attention."

"Nothing you've told me or shown me has contradicted anything I got from my teacher. You have, however, embellished much of it...a lot."

"If we ever get around to you experiencing sexual relations as a woman, Wu, it'll be a long time from now with a step-by-step process to get there."

"We're talking about sex as the ancients held it in a particularly cultivated context."

"Yes, and many graduated steps we don't even have names for in modern languages."

"Girls, not women, falling in love with other girls in an atmosphere of encouragement. It's intriguing. And this is while they're learning how to walk in and out of fire and stuff like that."

"Yeah, you can see how that might alter your view of sex."

Memory:
Another Lifetime,
Another Place

*I feel life is so small unless it has windows
into other worlds.*
~ Bertrand Russell

That evening Wu sank into an unusually deep sleep. Sometime in the middle of night, he began what could have been a long dream. What it felt like was a greater reality, as if the person in the dream were the real Wu, and the previous Wu, the wandering Taoist, was the dream or perhaps an imposter.

She was about thirteen and feeling those first stirrings in her body that felt delightful at times and sometimes made her feel crazy and out of control. She was still a girl who loved her dolls and her mother, but she also felt like running through the woods with no particular destination, just the desire to run and keep running with wild abandon and a strangely different but growing faith in herself.

She had a friend. They had played together for as long as either could remember. They were rough and tumble girls who could equally get into something like a formal tea party with all the accoutrements including the laughter that couldn't be contained.

One day they were hugging as they always had done, when there arose a desire to somehow be closer. Wu stood back and matter-of-factly asked, "You wanna kiss?"

Ariel, the other girl, laid a finger on her cheek as if deep in thought. She often did that and was usually joking, not thinking about anything. "All right," she replied just as matter-of-factly. But then they moved closer together and felt a pleasant warmth. "All kinda melty," they described it later.

Wu leaned toward the other girl, who reciprocated. They pressed together lip to lip, then began exploring, nibbling and licking, taking possession of the other's lips and tongue. Wu stepped back holding Ariel's hand and gazing fondly into her eyes. "I want you, in a way I've never felt before."

"Me too."

"Let's sit." And so they did, there in a grassy meadow full of flowers.

Wu pulled the other girl to her, to sit on her lap and wrap her legs around Wu's waist. They continued kissing and stroking each other's backsides. Neither had been touched exactly like this before. They were touching with love but also an urge to merge, to get ever closer, to feel the Oneness. And they were feeling the Oneness more and more, while tenderly discovering the formerly hidden parts of themselves.

Ariel loved the sensation of Wu's moist mouth against hers, slowly sliding lips over lips, tongue exploring tongue. Utter delight coursed through them as they continued to kiss and touch. Wu licked Ariel's neck and cheeks. The other girl let out a breathy moan of sensual glee. Wu continued until Ariel did the same back to her. "I couldn't contain it any longer. I had to give some back."

Wu pulled her arms out of her blouse so her shoulders were bare. Ariel did the same, so that they could also lick each other's shoulders and chest. "You're so soft," Ariel exclaimed.

"Your tongue is so soft."

Running fingers through each other's hair, they held each other's cheeks, gazing into the grotto of each other's eyes. "You're so deep," Ariel declared and then giggled.

"Come into my depths, my darling." Laughter burst from both of them before subsiding into more symphonies of mmm and ahhh.

They began to toy and play with their sensuality, for instance running a finger lightly along some skin ordinarily not touched and watching for the inevitable wave of pleasure in each other's eyes.

"I love you."

"I love you."

"I could stay like this forever."

"So could I, but we should probably go home for dinner. We can come back."

"Yeah, when we're better prepared with a picnic and a blanket."

"And lots of chocolate." They squealed their delight, the mischievous little girls again.

Somehow in this dream, or was it a dream, Wu knew they would come back many times and go together to other places as well, and never tire of the touch of the other eliciting little waves of ecstasy.

And Daphne was somehow the calm observer of Wu and his girlfriend. Actually not exactly calm, perhaps bemused, mostly enjoying Wu learning about something so well known to her. Otherwise she might never have survived high school. She awoke from an apparent nap in the back seat of the jeep in a state of sympathetic amusement, that was how she affirmed it later. She had not been physical or romantic with anyone for more than two years. She wondered if that would change when they got to Calabasas. She did not even know if any of her lovers were there.

The jeep was slowing down. "I'm not doing that," Atsa declared.

"What's happening?" the women asked in unison.

Then they all saw the tiny sign and arrow. The sign said, "Chaco." Not even a road, literally two tire tracks meandering in the direction of nearby hills. The tire tracks ended abruptly at the narrow mouth of a canyon. Sheer walls disappeared into the hills.

"Let's sit and hold hands," Daphne suggested. An obviously different consciousness came over all of them. They had seen a canyon like this before. It would open up into...they knew not what, likely to its own unique unfolding mystery.

"Bring provisions," a voice murmured. "The shamans of Chaco came here to be more fully immersed in the womb of Mother Earth." As abruptly as it had begun, the voice ended. The three friends regarded their compatriots, nodded their agreement and began to prepare for their journey.

The walls were sheer, but oddly moist to the touch, though there was no running water to be seen. They could walk easily, but there was no more space than that and a blue patch of sky above. Soon the walls and floor became almost greasy. They could not hold their footing and soon were sliding along comfortably on their butts. Light became darkness; the sky disappeared; downhill they went deep into the earth. Something between a thrill ride and a genuine rebirth. A chamber, soft glow of liquid amethyst, shining and sparkling, each one emanating a mild wave of pleasure.

Daphne remembered all her lovers and friends in the Goddess Circle. Aiyana felt herself being held by Grandmother as she had when Aiyana was younger. Atsa was out with the sheep as a boy. There was a visitation by a light being, who felt like family, perfectly safe and filled to overflowing with the love that radiates from Her Oneness. They all felt a pervasive blessing as they continued their slide ever deeper into dark-ness and its own special light. A spectral vision from the be-ings that dwell in this Holy Darkness, that we might see and know and feel their dark beauty as our own, a collective birth-right of holy ecstasy. They all reached out to send blessings to all their beloveds.

A soft light suffused the ground beneath and the air above as they emerged into a valley of soft grass, so inviting they luxuriated in newfound visual and sensual pleasures until they felt themselves totally relaxed on a bed of the lightest feathers. When someone did appear and greet them it hardly disrupted the liquid warmth that seemed to flow through them.

"We can converse, and it will not disrupt the flow," she said, as if she was reading their thoughts. "I am Anaya. Just think of me as a big sister. No need to introduce yourselves. We know who you are. I am curious about your first impres-sions of our place."

In a dreamy, drifty voice Daphne murmured, "Very pleas-ant."

"Can we stay?" Atsa asked.

"For a while."

"You *are* my big sister." Aiyana was glowing.

"Everything's so soft, the grass, the light, even the air. I love your color scheme." Daphne chuckled.

The landscape was almost as surreal as an abstract paint-ing. A lovely radiance emanated from everything including Anaya. "Float with me," she told them, and they did float with her toward that disappearing point in the painting where all the lines converge. Anaya reached out her hands, and they all held hands as they drifted along so peacefully.

Anaya began to explain: "This place is like no other place. We are all individuals here, so much so that we rarely see each other, but the lines of power that run between us keep us in-timately connected. We feel one another all the time like a hive or an ant colony. We have always lived in the earth like this.

People from the surface have lived with us. Many still visit, though less and less until recently."

"Visit? I feel like we were called here," Aiyana declared.

Anaya laughed. "You know the word visitation. Who is visiting whom? You are here partly because you have prepared yourself to be present with us."

"What's the other part?"

Anaya laughed again. "We have been observing you and recognizing your progress. There are many more like you again. Many places around our Mother."

"You are connected with all of them?"

"Yes, it's kind of like a computer network except the network is the expanding neural pathways of our brains and minds. We can tune in and get impressions from the other side of the world."

"Are there pathways in the earth," Atsa asked.

"Oh yes, She is the radiating center of our matrix."

"I can see it. Lines criss-crossing all through her body," Daphne declared.

"Through Her we can touch everyone and feel the love, a genuine intimacy thousands of miles away, but still part of Her body, a neuron in touch with all the other neurons."

"Lovely."

They had passed beyond the disappearing point into an area that appeared to be rolling hills, just large enough to recline on. They settled among the hills that were soft like foam.

"In this place we are simply living in the Oneness. We don't have to do anything to make it happen. We don't do ceremonies or rituals or shamanic practices, because they're not necessary. The efforts you make on the surface of Our Mother are necessary to draw to you more of that Oneness energy. Here we are steeped in it. We are closer to the center of Her matrix."

"So what do you do?" Aiyana asked.

"We exist. We float. Sometimes we make up games. We

might have to temporarily erect barriers toward reading each other. Mostly we are in a flow of heart energy, Heart of the Mother, and we let it carry us wherever She takes us. The handful of times when we've had lots of refugees from the surface, somehow many of us showed up and knew what we needed to do, instruments of our Mother, who is not so much a conductor, as a radiance from heart and womb, multiple swirls carousing out of that molten ether endlessly generating gold and silver and rainbows to create and reconcile She is never destroyed. She can be injured, injured badly enough that humans cannot sustain life on the surface while she heals.

"We all know that apparent destruction is all part of the process. Fire burns the dry forest to make way for new growth. Of course there have been long periods of time when people on the surface lived much as we live here, balance and flow. No need for such major destruction."

"The garden?"

"So to speak, though there are better stories of the Garden."

"So what happened?"

"It was a slow drift away from the blessings of the Mother. The lust for power. The desire to individually make dramatic things happen. It's a thrill. Children come into that when they're two and three years old, boys more than girls, getting fascinated with outward strength. The feminine strength has always been about the magical ability to give birth. When there were first men, they were good boys, choir boys, they put their outward energy into creative pursuits. Bisexual mating, that came later, another experiment."

"You think we're a failed experiment," Atsa asked.

"Not exactly, we're still viewing the male as a work in progress."

"That includes me?"

"You've made tremendous progress; your deeper understanding has grown from the time of your healing, where you met these friends."

"Yes, when I went home magical things kept happening, contact with spirit beings, having conversations with animals, feeling like I could almost fly, losing parts of days and not knowing where I'd been."

"Wow," Aiyana exclaimed. She and Atsa looked into each other's eyes for just a few seconds, but it was enough to see the Mother in the other and remember that was what initially drew them together.

"'When you live in the flow, there's no need for weapons,'" Daphne quoted. She had felt what passed between Aiyana and Atsa. She wanted to say something but chose not to.

There was a long pause before Leilani softly insisted, "Say it." Anaya's name had changed almost imperceptibly. Atsa was the only one who noticed and wondered.

Daphne collected herself for a moment and turned to Atsa and Aiyana. "I'm honored and touched in an intimate way to be in the presence of your sweet love. I feel it in my heart. I feel it in my womb. It tickles my entire being in just the right way."

Rather than blushing or squirming, the young couple took in Daphne's words. Aiyana replied first. "I know you see me and I love being seen by you. And now you see Atsa and me, and you know us."

Atsa looked at Aiyana, grinned and shrugged before turning to Daphne. "You are a very special person. We met in the Spirit World, at least that's where I was." Daphne nodded. "You were this angel who flew into my heart with some kind of fairy dust. Your beautiful blond curly hair streaming behind you. We were in space somewhere, and you flew in and out of my heart a few times."

Aiyana looked at Atsa and then back to Daphne. "And your shining bright blue eyes lighting a path for all of us."

Not much was said for a while. The group meandered into

a dreamy reverie. There had been no mention of food nor water, yet they weren't hungry or thirsty.

"All of that is suspended for now." Leilani read their thoughts. "Sorry it's what we do hear, but like I said, I can turn it off." She looked around. Everyone was emphatically shaking their heads. "We're in control of a lot of things. One of those is bodily needs. We can suspend them for a while."

"You must have done that for us," Atsa stated.

"It's like a field. We're all in the field. We can eat anytime. We do enjoy food. We don't need it like people do on the surface."

"You're our guide," Aiyana asserted.

"Nothing more need be said," Atsa added.

"So you just float around here most of the time?" Aiyana asked when the conversation began again.

"Pretty much." Leilani laughed. "Our work is not nearly so much on the physical plane like it is on the surface. My main responsibility along with many others is maintaining a network, keeping all the circuits activated, here, but also the matrix extends to the surface. There have been many disruptions of the signal."

"Disruptions?" Daphne looked for clarification.

"Wars, famines, eco-disasters. Violence blocks our com lines. We can't get through. Long ago we looked and felt more like one family. We went back and forth. Life on the surface was much like it is here, now. In these later times it's special for your world to have communion with ours. There is an us and them. You seek through prayer and meditation and ceremony to call in the spiritual healing, and under the best of circumstances our love can touch you and heal you. You have experienced these things."

"So the things that Grandmother Xochitl and others teach are important," Aiyana asserted.

"Very important, it opens the door or keeps the door open so that things beyond the physical can heal the physical."

"So you're behind all this," said Atsa with a sly smile.

"Many of us compose this level of the Holy Matrix, constantly giving birth no matter how much destruction is let loose up there. You are among those who choose to give birth with us."

"How did things get so bad on the surface?" Daphne asked. "You said it used to be as peaceful and full of love as it is here."

"It was unintentional. It took a long time, a very slow drift away from the matrix into uncharted territory. The exploration was fine at first, you know, climbing mountains, swimming in oceans, shape-shifting, of course. All in good fun. Somebody thought it was fun to have a sky god to cavort with some emanation of the Mother. Nothing wrong with that until some got clever and declared the sky god to be superior to Earth Mother and therefore had the right to dominate her."

"Superior, on what basis?" Daphne was almost irate.

Leilani looked almost impish as she replied. "You may have noticed we do not have fire here. We have no need of it. There is a radiance we can call on at any moment to provide heat, but because our bodies are also quite adjustable, it's not an everyday need. On the surface there is fire, and where does fire come from?"

"The sky," Atsa replied.

"Yes, lightning lights fires. Everything else is imitation of that. Sky god, thunderbolt god, is dramatic, powerful, dangerous and sometimes destructive. Increasingly there was emphasis on physical power, competitions, tests of strength, boyish fun until it got taken too seriously, the power of domination superseding the power of cooperation. Stand alone with muscle and metal. What matrix?" She paused and looked around herself. The rolling hills still resembled an impressionist painting. "But enough talk. Let me show you what we like to do here."

Leilani slowly ascended. "Watch me once, then you can do it." She started with cartwheels but soon was soaring like a bird, banking her turns, describing circles and spirals that emitted something like rainbow fairy dust. It sparkled, tiny crystals in the sky or whatever this atmosphere was called down here.

Soon the three friends were flying with Leilani. They were birds that were trick-riding ponies and Peking Opera acrobats. Flying so easily as a unified flock, a small murmuration, the energy that unified them more powerful than the energy that separated them. A convocation of doves, they were effortless and tireless.

They weren't really tired, just feeling like flowing into another activity. They reclined again like integral parts of the landscape. Leilani seemed to be speaking directly to the memory banks of their brains. "People need to know: God loves you; Goddess loves you; Your Holy Mother loves you; these are not just empty concepts. She literally is our Mother and is constantly giving birth to new creations. Mothers literally fall in love with their newborns. It could even be called infant worship. It is full-throttle and unconditional. She loves each of us like we are that newborn infant propelling dopamine and oxytocin and other feel-good brain chemicals to sustain that mother love."

"Is there anything similar in men?" Atsa asked.

"Not really, though men who are open to it can experience something similar to maternal-infant bonding. In the modern world they have to want it and to value it. Otherwise the macho posturing and demeaning of the feminine, which is built into the fabric of modern society, will erode their ability to maintain such a loving attitude."

A line of thought was stimulated in Daphne. "So Anaya, for women it's unavoidable to feel this Holy Mother Love even with the harshness of modern society discouraging such extremely feminine traits. For men, they have to work at it with the opposition of other men and a society that exalts the male over the female in the form of warriors and kings and others who play domination games."

"Yes, if we're going to have world peace and loving communities, men have to get over the fear of being called sissies and allow themselves the love that occurs naturally if a bunch of make-believe impediments are not put in the way."

"So you're describing societies where men are not afraid to be more like women." Aiyana summarized for herself.

"And, therefore, can be among the loving minions of She, who constantly manifests and sustains the Oneness of all creation, so we may live and be blessed."

"When we return to the surface," Daphne asked, "how do we carry this?"

"You already do. We brought you here to let you know that what you have been living and teaching is the truth, as we know it to be. You have our support in these times to propagate these understandings by whatever means you have available to you. For men to trust that they can lay down their arms, and that will foster a better outcome than all of this mythological battle between good and evil."

Atsa declared, "The battle itself is evil and it produces more evil, more destruction, more human misery. There are no winners in war, only those who are less damaged."

And Daphne wondered out loud. "But how do we get the patriarchal know-it-alls to give up one of their core beliefs. Even their Bible is full of battles, the righteous thumping those who are less than *chosen*."

Anaya/Leilani had a simple answer. "Our enclaves will expand, and the patriarchs will do what they feel they need to do to each other."

"Does Holy Mother still love them?" Aiyana asked.

"Oh yes, just like a mother who loves a tyrannical three-year-old and hopes he will get over his temper tantrum sometime soon."

Completing the Circle

Life is a full circle, widening until it joins
the circle motions of the infinite.
~ Anais Nin

Never settle in any circle that is not fully
committed to forever walk in the direction
of endless opportunities and possibilities.
~ Edmond Mbiaka

Back on the road, two young women and one young man knew they were nearing the community of Calabasas. Daphne wondered how different it would be from the last time she was there more than two years ago. She reflected that her travels with Wu had not only strengthened her practice and her teaching skills. They had been guided into a world where they had begun to learn the ways of shamans and develop a level of expertise and a growing sense of confidence in their skills and attunement.

When they drove the dirt road to the parking area of the growing village, Daphne noticed that there were more adobe structures and a bustle of people seeming to act with purpose near midday of a relatively cool day. A lone young woman approached to greet the newcomers. It was Viv, and she had definitely traversed the passage of puberty.

"Daphne, is that you?" she yelled from a distance.

In answer Daphne waved both arms and did a little dance. As Viv drew near, Daphne exclaimed, "You're beautiful. You're a lovely young woman."

"Should I blush?" she joked. "Where have you been, and where's Wu?"

"One question at a time. We've been wandering. Wu is getting some advanced training at another site. Let me introduce my newer friends, Aiyana and Atsa."

Before Viv could respond, Aiyana declared, "You're as old as I am."

"I'm told I look quite mature for my age. I act kinda grown up too, and I'm educated way beyond my years."

"Me too. We met Daphne quite a ways east of here. We've received messages that it's time to be here now."

"Others have arrived recently with similar stories. We are glad we have steadily built beyond current needs. So far everyone is housed between here and the portal encampment. People tend to rotate in and out of there.

"So the portal is happening?" Daphne queried. "It was only being talked about when we left. Is it a circle of yurts like we talked about?"

"Not always a circle now, but plenty of yurts."

Daphne watched another woman approach and could not tell if it was Nan or her soul-sister Nina. She walked directly to Daphne and gave her a big warm hug and offered the same to Atsa and Aiyana. They accepted and reciprocated.

"I love meeting people this way, no names, no words exchanged, but I know you're family."

"Where's that wise little girl, Nan?" Daphne had to satisfy her curiosity about the genius spirit being, who'd been born to Nina and the community at large.

"Oh, she's around somewhere. She knows her way around and doesn't stray far. She's a pre-teen in a three-year-old body."

"Yes, I'm definitely here." They all heard her as if she was standing among them. Daphne and Nan exchanged an amused look.

"And her mother?" Daphne continued.

"Nina floats between here and the portal. More accurately she rides her horse. She seems to float because of all the time she spends with the air beings. Everyone helps out with Flor. She doesn't need much, especially now that she's so mobile and capable of rustling up some food if she needs to."

Then they saw her coming their way from a direction outside the main village. She was holding something. As she drew near, they could see she had a rabbit. The rabbit appeared totally at peace. Flor paused a few yards away. "Manifest your peace," she commanded in her little girl voice.

The group each went inside themselves to comply with her request, and Flor closed the distance between them. "This is Ella," she explained. "She hasn't had a litter yet. Her mother and I were friends, too. Sometimes we have to hide from coyotes, but that comes natural if you're a rabbit. We learn from each other."

Daphne knelt down and reached her arms toward Flor. The three of them came together in a gentle hug. "I'm just delighted to see you, Flor."

"I'm delighted too."

"Are you still speaking for the spirit beings?"

"Yes," she began tentatively. "My friends from the other world..." She looked to Nan who continued the explanation, while Flor petted her rabbit and smiled beatifically.

"We've had to limit the public channelings. We were starting to get overwhelmed by curiosity-seekers. Outsiders may come once a week for a formal public channeling and may ask questions. We also have an evening community meeting once a week to keep our process on track and headed in the right direction."

Atsa exercised his curiosity. "I am intrigued by this portal you mentioned. I don't know what that is. It sounds important."

Flor spoke up. "My friends from the other world, the sky beings and air beings need a place to be when the big changes start to happen. They need a place where they can enter our world and be safe. Mommy Nina and I ride her horse to the portal once or twice a week. Sometimes we sleep there. Sometimes we take a pack horse or a mule with supplies. Sometimes the angels and sylphs visit while we're there."

The three travelers spent the night in the only empty building. For now it accommodated recently arrived guests until they made other arrangements or departed. Feeling pleasantly full from their first home-cooked meal in some time, they were ready for sleep early in the evening. Flor had other ideas. She stayed behind when the others left. Nan assured them, "She sometimes stays the night where she chooses. Her telepathy keeps us aware of where she is."

Flor settled in and let Ella, the rabbit, scamper around the dirt floor. The travelers were still camping out, this time with adobe walls and a solid roof. "Don't worry," Flor told them. "You can go to sleep. I will sleep too. My sky friends will probably visit, but it will be like a dream." She turned to Daphne. "May I sleep with you?"

"Of course."

Nothing that dramatic occurred during the night. They were with winged spirit beings as if floating on a cloud while simultaneously feeling that there was something solid underneath them. They sat in a circle interspersed with their sky friends, as if sitting in council. The content was unclear. The sense of sitting in a circle of equals was unmistakable. The connection was powerful, the love almost overwhelming. Flor flew among the others, a little fairy scattering sparkles wherever she went.

In the morning Nina appeared with horses for all of them packed with provisions for the journey and the portal camp. It was uncanny how Nina looked like a slightly younger, slightly more beautiful version of her cousin, Nan. She went immediately to Daphne, lay down beside her and enclosed her and Flor in a long warm leisurely hug. Then she withdrew enough to look at her old friend. "So absolutely delightful to see you. While we ride today, you must tell me about your journeys. I'll try to catch you up on so much that has happened here."

By way of response Daphne rose up and kissed her on the lips. "It's all been quite fascinating, but I have missed my friends and lovers."

Aiyana and Atsa were sitting up in their sleeping bags. Nina sat in front of each of them in turn and extended a long warm hug. "We are some of your family," she stated simply. "It's a blessing for all of us that you are here. And you're so young. That's an added bonus."

Aiyana replied, "Flor is here, and we met Viv last night."

"Yes, your amazing maturity for your years fits right in here. Viv will go with us. She's holding the horses for our early start."

"Wonderful."

"And Josh, who is about your age." She turned to Atsa. "He knows the animals and plants around here about as well as anybody."

In a few minutes they had partaken of enough sustenance and were on their horses headed for higher elevation. Nina led with Flor in front of her on the saddle, and Josh followed behind the rest of the group. Atsa sought him out when the terrain permitted them to ride side by side. They looked at each other, intuitively discerning a long-lost brother. Indeed, they were both quite knowledgeable about their surroundings. They exchanged English and Navajo names for the distant mountains. Atsa spoke of what he knew about their significance in Navajo ceremonial tradition. Josh pointed out various plants and some of their uses.

Viv told Aiyana, "I know I'm about to become a woman. It can't have been that long ago for you. Tell me what you think I should know."

Aiyana laughed. "Is everyone at Calabasas as direct as you are?"

Viv chuckled. "Pretty much. No false modesty here."

"Probably the first requirement for a medicine woman. It's hard to prepare anyone. You'll feel things you've never felt before, in your body and in your emotions. Other feelings will be more intense than they've ever been before."

"I think that's already starting."

"It doesn't last forever, but at first it's pretty dramatic."

"You will see," Nina said to Daphne. "The portal camp is a real settlement. Calabasas has grown. Friends visit, and some know they're supposed to be here and return to be members of the community. You probably saw all the building we've been doing. The construction company is busy at Calabasas and other sites which generate income for our own building program. Some of us, like me, are fortunate to be liaisons and packers between the two sites. I've had a lot of time with our sky friends. They are very light-hearted about everything that's going on. Their motto seems to be, 'Be of good cheer.' There is no doom and gloom about the coming changes, just energy and enthusiasm to help us keep going in the right direction. What about you?"

"We lived in the camp of an amazing medicine woman for many months, learned so much. Then we felt the pull to come here. Along the way there were a number of forays into the Other World. My young friends have been more than equal partners. Wu was called to stay at one of the settlements that spans the two worlds. I'm sure we'll see him again, but it might be a while."

"And before the medicine woman?"

"We wandered and taught the Taoist Way."

The trail reached a broad flat expanse within the surrounding mountains. In the central area the dirt was packed hard as if trodden by many feet. Yurts and other semi-permanent structures dotted the surrounding landscape. They were greeted by a woman Daphne vaguely remembered from before. Her name was Shaylin, and she was one of the dozen or so who lived here in the portal village most of the time, so that visitors could feel at home. "Of course you're here for the weekly ceremony," she said to Nina, "and it looks like you've brought us lots of provisions."

"Of course," Nina replied having led the horses to a place for unloading. Others arrived to help organize and arrange the goods in one of the larger yurts. Among them was Asherah, whom Daphne remembered from the Goddess Circle in Northern California.

"Ash," she called out and went to her with open arms, hugging her long-lost sister. They looked into each other's eyes in silent acknowledgment of all that they had shared.

Shaylin addressed the newcomers. "Tomorrow is our weekly ceremony. It is a blessing to us all each time. For now it is why we're here." She looked directly at Atsa and couldn't resist saying, "You must be a very special young man."

"He is," Daphne and Aiyana answered in unison.

Viv took Atsa and Aiyana to a smaller yurt, whose interior clearly showed an artistic feminine touch. When they had deposited their personal belongings, they rejoined the others. Shaylin told them, "Feel free to wander around. Nothing is really off limits. Outside of the settled area we are actually in kind of an ecological paradise. The variety of flora and fauna is quite impressive as are some of the rock formations. In a few hours we'll have an evening meal, but there are snacks over there in the kitchen yurt."

"We brought some fresh fruit and vegetables," Viv chimed

in.

"A few women are currently camping solo. They'll return in a few days to tell us their latest discoveries and revelations. That's kind of our existence, lots of time to attune ourselves to the larger themes of the universe." Shaylin smiled warmly.

Atsa was wondering if there were any other men around, when Flor exclaimed, "Daddy," and rushed in the direction of a man coming their way. She jumped in his arms like any little girl might.

"My sweet girl," Will murmured in her ear as she celebrated being in his arms. "Any words of wisdom for us."

Flor laughed. "Maybe later, Daddy."

"Flor is often an added attraction to our contemplations," Shaylin stated casually.

"You're such a good audience," the little girl teased.

"Would you show us around?" Atsa asked Viv.

"Sure," Viv replied. "Come with me." She led them to the edge of the settlement where they could already see a rich lush wild garden extending into the distance. There was a broad trail through all the greenery. Viv extended a hand to each of them. "You're my new brother and sister," she declared. Soon they were skipping down the trail together, quite delighted to be where they were.

The next morning began with a leisurely emergence from sleeping accommodations to partake in a casual breakfast. There were a few offhand references to this impending day of ceremony with the sky beings who were now like old friends or family, reliably showing up to share an ongoing cultivation of vision with their Earth sisters and brothers. With the recent arrivals the earth group numbered close to twenty. With the warmth of mid-morning they arranged themselves in an approximate circle in meditative posture expectantly awaiting the arrival of the winged spirit beings.

A vortex gradually appeared above them, obviously a passageway for the angels and sylphs who slowly descended, almost floated down, to take places alternating with their earth sisters and brothers. With a remarkable symmetry the circle precisely alternated earth people and sky people. As soon as everyone was settled, an aura of golden light arose around and above them. Most surprising to the newcomers, they could feel themselves rising from their seats on the earth. The space below filled with golden light such that the group of forty individuals were entirely suffused, and the surrounding landscape was no longer visible.

They could see the earth, as if they had risen to a vantage point far above. Then the visions began and unfolded almost like watching a movie. Like eagles they could see the entire expanse and also focus in on components of the panorama and see them in clear detail. Somehow they could even see the far sides of the earth. Numerous mushroom-shaped clouds arose from every region of inhabited earth. Close-up focus showed scenes of fire and ash. People, buildings, plants and animals had been instantly incinerated. If anything was untouched, it was the polar regions and isolated area in the large oceans. What might have been terrifying under ordinary circumstances was incorporated into a meditative calm that pervaded the group, even the first-timers.

Oddly dispassionate and contemplative as if on a meditation retreat, the group merely observed as the scenes of destruction by fire faded out to be replaced by an earth where the oceans had risen and expanded. Much of the previous land mass was under water including all coastal cities and other installations including docking facilities for ships, oil installations and power plants.

As the visions continued, the group felt quite safe and separate from what was transpiring below them. Less visually dramatic but just as pervasive were the images of a global pandemic. Focusing in on various locations around the earth the images were strikingly similar: more people were sick, dying and dead than there were any obviously healthy individuals. Infrastructure was rapidly deteriorating so that those not devastated by the deadly microbes were succumbing to starvation, exposure to extreme weather and the rampages of those driven insane by the traumatic conditions.

Perhaps connected to the pandemic were scenes of heavily armed gangs roaming the countryside to secure for themselves the necessities of life. There were inevitable fatalities as those with guns found the need to use them. In some cases it was clear that cannibalism was being practiced, and those without guns became the prey of those who were armed.

There were also scenes of enclaves, much like the ones that Daphne, Wu, Aiyana and Atsa had recently visited. In these parallel dimensions, a simple life ensued. Food was being grown, spiritual practices maintained, and some refugees taken in who were fleeing the destruction of the world but had some sense of a larger meaning to everything that was coming to pass. These enclaves were dots on a map of massive scale, but they existed in all areas of earth. The presence of sky beings was obvious in most of these enclaves.

Several hours elapsed as the people born of earth and those who hailed from the sky sat in a grand circle together, enclosed in a protective aura of golden light. There were successive scenes of possible futures. Some were apocalyptic; some felt more like a normal oscillation of cycles that had always been endemic to life on earth; some were gloriously rosy visions of utopian futures. To the earthlings the harmony and flow of these utopias seemed unreal, well-nigh impossible, certainly by the standards of the so-called modern world.

Often the humans in these utopias appeared quite comfortable without the construction of massive buildings and mechanical infrastructures. The humans were able to regulate themselves instead of devoting so much energy to regulating the environment. Daphne and her young friends had experienced this harmony and medicine power in the enclaves they had been drawn into.

Later Flor spoke to the group telepathically. Clearly she was a sky being, although born of earth parents. She had often said, "I am one of the first. There are more on the way." From before her birth she had been a medium for higher teachings that those around her could receive telepathically. Now in this context that was already an interface between earth and sky, her message reinforced what had already been transmitted via vision.

"So many possible futures. For now it is our role to attach to none of them, neither our grandest hopes nor our most terrible fears. This is our time of contemplation. That is our contribution to a more positive outcome, that we may sit in close proximity to perfect equanimity and serenity. Huge forces are in motion, pushing things one way and another. We are one of those forces but only one. Above all, have no fear. By doing what we are doing we are protected. Our circle of protection is expanding. Remember, no soul is lost. Even in the most horrendous of destructions, death is ultimately a peaceful transition, the first chapter in a new book, which may or may not result in rebirth on our Mother Earth as carbon-based biological organisms.

"Nothing is ever created or destroyed, one of your scientists said. Perhaps, but on the other hand we are in a constant process of destruction and creation. However, nothing is ever lost nor ceases to exist. Maybe that's what he meant. Meanwhile the rules of biological existence on earth are loosening again. What has been known as magic will again become commonplace. What is uncertain, what is still not clear is what path we will take to get there. Will it be the easy way or the hard way, a culling process or wholesale destruction? Whichever it turns out to be, we sit within the oneness and embrace the love we already know from those who have invited us into these places where the worlds mingle and cross-pollinate."

"What do they get from us?" It was a loud thought from

Aiyana.

"Have you ever loved a baby or a small child, who explores and experiments so freely? The delight of discovering something for the first time, we get to experience it with them. They make many mistakes. They fall down and hurt themselves. We do not judge them. We simply keep trying to show them a better way. Our elders in other worlds are like good parents. At our worst, our craziest, our most destructive, we are a joy to them. Their love is unconditional.

"As you observe the potential for destruction that lies ahead, it is natural to fear the inevitable loss. We are here to reassure you that as you transition into a higher level of understanding, you will know that nothing is ever really gained or lost. Things change and transform, but they do not cease to be. All the loving connections you have formed remain with you. This can be difficult to remember when all around you are scenes of death and destruction. We, your heavenly parents, are always with you. The bond you have formed with everyone you have loved is also imperishable, even when there are long periods of separation, such as happens with physical death. Increasingly you will be able to reach out with your minds to nurture and enjoy those connections in the same way you have used your telepathy to connect those who are physically separated from you, such as living on the other side of the world. The more that you love someone the easier it is to connect with them telepathically."

Nina remembered how powerfully she and Will had remained connected only weeks after they had gotten together. She was in Paris doing her semester abroad, while he had returned to his teaching job in California. They had done everything telepathically, including making love.

Flor continued: "Most have journeyed into other worlds, other dimensions, the many mansions of our Earth Mother's house. Some have begun to explore the vast realms of sky. Matrices of interconnection expanding ever outward, we will never reach a finite edge. For now we will nurture and strengthen these places where we come together as beings of earth and sky. So many wonders await us as we complete one earth cycle as best we can. We are charitable toward those who've blindly or even knowingly taken the path toward destruction. This earth cycle has tested humans' ability to maintain the eternal truths in the face of extreme adversity. Some of you have done better than others. Everyone has the opportunity to move on, not just the 'A' students."

A telepathic chuckle passed through the group. Some relaxed a bit as they remembered friends and relatives who had thus far been unable to tune into the higher truths. Good to know they were still eligible for seats on the Ark.

"Yes, the Ark of the Covenant," Flor continued. "The promise is real. The opportunity to evolve is always available, no matter how long it takes for some to see and accept the truth."

A spontaneous wave of love arose in the group in recognition of the intimate sense of creative connection which Flor had just described. Each of these weekly ceremonies had brought the earthlings ever closer in their hearts and minds to their sisters and brothers from the sky. Flor's channeled commentary put words around nascent and half-formed feelings that were finding room to endlessly bloom, each person a flower opening up, and opening up from an apparently infinite center.

Epilogue

The real ceremony begins where the formal one
ends, when we take up a new way, our minds and
hearts filled with the vision of earth that holds us
within it, in compassionate relationship
to and with our world.
~ Linda Hogan

Nina had taken to riding farther away from the settlement at Calabasas and exploring further into the surrounding wilderness. Usually her only companion was her chestnut paint, a younger mare she'd only had a couple of years. Flor was such a child of the community that almost anyone would be happy to have her for a day and see it as a good deal. Occasionally Will would come with Nina. He was quite immersed in the adobe construction company which had expanded considerably and had many folks wanting their services. Sometimes Flor accompanied her mother and jabbered combinations of wisdom and gibberish from her tandem saddle. Her balance was already quite good.

Occasionally she visited the portal, but everything there was going well without her particularly having a role or responsibility. Something had drawn her into wanting to know the land more intimately. Flor sometimes made vague pronouncements like, "They're waiting for you out there."

When Nina asked, "Who? Who's waiting for me?"

Flor answered telepathically, "You'll know them."

So Nina was committed to a quest and a promise of connection with something important.

Flor was somewhat disarming as a three-year-old. She was in most ways a normal three-year-old who loved to play, loved silliness, laughed a lot and delighted those around her. And then there was this voice of profound wisdom which had begun her telepathic pronouncements when she was still in utero. This voice knew so much more than the little girl who embodied her. Did they even talk to each other or was Flor simply an open channel?

Today Nina rode alone and felt strongly connected to all the life around her as if it were one living breathing organism and she was an integrated part of this magnificent organism. Since the family had moved from Northern California, otherworldly perceptions and experiences had become more common than ever. She began to expect to have contact with beneficent spirits from the other world. They felt almost casual.

As her explorations led her to ever higher elevations, she always traveled prepared in case something happened and she was forced to spend the night. So she was not especially surprised when a very clear voice in the middle of the day directed her to stop where a flat outcropping projected from the vague trail she was following, and a broad finger pointed to the east. The day was warm, and she had ridden far beyond her usual parameters, but was quite drawn to do so.

At the base of the finger, she sat against an upright rock and drifted into something between sleep and meditation; a lovely lilting rhythm played in her body as she opened herself to further guidance. For many minutes there was only the rhythm that seemed to take her deeper into a mysterious but pleasant darkness from which a small flame spoke to her: "It is time for you to know us more intimately. Collect wood so you may have a small fire that lasts all night. In the meantime, bask in the soft sensuality of this delicious darkness." Then the flame was gone and Nina felt herself held like an infant with a sense of total immersion in the flesh and radiance of some larger female being.

When Nina emerged, as if being slowly squeezed out of that loving darkness, she noticed the shadows had lengthened considerably. She gazed into the distance, where the sun kissed the bright white snow on far-flung peaks. She still had several hours to collect wood and wandered back among the trees which clustered to the west of her.

Soon she had carried and dragged an adequate pile close to a depression near the fingertip. Each time she walked the length of the finger she felt like she was walking into open space, like this fire would be suspended in air. She snacked on fresh-cut vegetables from the community garden and home-made hummus, and wondered out loud what they had in store for her this night.

She wrote in her journal:

Beings of the other world
  my friends
How did I live before I knew you?
  and they answered.
You always had your intuition
  only now you know from whence it comes

She laughed as she wrote the last line. "How simple it is," she thought, "yet utterly profound when we first realize." The whole sky was turning shades of pink as the sun behind her sank toward the western horizon.

Nina stepped into the fire she had laid. It was a doorway. She immediately stepped out of the fire into another world. It was a world of water. She was not clear if she was immersed in the water, but she was breathing normally. Everything was in shades of blues and greens. There was a light source somewhere above, but it was muted. Everything shimmered, coalesced in waves and scattered time and again. There was a voice in her head. It was her voice, but it was telling a story.

"The people still lived in the rivers back then. We were all undines, our natural state of being. Days were spent swimming about or resting in a still pool, clambering about the rivulets and tributaries, but never straying too far from the flow and rush of water. Did we have adventures and explorations? Oh, yes, and the rivers, the arteries of Mother Earth were ever-changing. The storms of a winter would chart new courses, wash away land and toss logs into the waterways. We often swam together in synchronous beauty, sharing and showing moves that made our dance ever more a liquid mandala. Rushing among the rushes, an intricate slalom, or relaxing in warm springs, it was all good."

As the voice continued its description of a time so ancient and pure, Nina relaxed into an immersive fulfillment, as if she were in a constant state of baptism. "What a paltry remnant," she thought. "At one time our entire existence was suffused with water. It was the essence of pure spirit, and it was the world we lived in. Now our religions imply that a one-time immersion or even a sprinkling of water on the forehead is adequate to keep us connected with spirit. It feels so easy to just live in the water most of the time, never to stray very far." Then she swam and danced and cavorted in the water, simultaneously a child at play and a well-tempered elder enveloped in the natural spirit of water.

As she swam on in the flow of peace and joy provided by the river of life which held her in its loving embrace, she noticed that there were other beings swimming with her, each one uniquely adapted for travel or suspension in this liquid home. They all appeared to be ensconced in the easy current of a medium-sized river, floating along from one indeterminate space and place to another. Nothing was very substantial, that is, everything was constantly changing including her own body. Sometimes she sprouted fins in place of or in addition to her arms. When she temporarily became a narwhal, she laughed as she saw herself as a sea-going unicorn.

The movements of the other water beings coalesced into an intricate yet apparently effortless dance. "An underwater murmuration," Nina declared and chuckled again, as her string of discoveries continued. "A school of water beings," she further declared, as one particular being glided into her immediate space. She found this water sprite particularly beautiful, large dark-blue eyes shone from a face of lighter blue and the protuberant mouth of a fish that somehow fit her face perfectly. Undulating filaments streamed from above both eyes. Suspended in front of Nina's eyes she radiated a deep but casual and comfortable love, as if Nina had been already recognized as a beloved but long-lost relative, whose presence brought joy to her assembled family.

As this sister drifted away, Nina followed occasionally swishing her tail to propel herself. They reached a sandy beach. Nina followed her new sister's lead and reclined upon the sand. The warmth of the sun was as pleasant as the coolness of the water had been. Telepathically she heard, "Yes, there was a time when we all lived this way in a natural harmony with all other beings, particularly those of the water. All existed in this magnificent balance, which we took for granted until something happened. A being appeared who was alien to the natural harmony of our lives. For thousands of years we had experienced nothing like the narrow-minded selfishness of these new beings. We know not where they came from or how they came to exist. We assumed there must be some dark sector of the universe which had previously been unknown to us, but that was only a theory. Gradually the expansive freedom we had always known began to constrict. Life was no longer entirely safe. We water beings, who had always been here, became prey for those of the crazy new way.

"That was so long ago, it's hard to imagine a world not dominated by those who practice violence and destruction and believe it is integral to their survival. What we perceived as a crazy new way has become the definition of normal. Those who teach the old ways are revered, but it has increasingly become empty lip service. The principles of Jesus and others are still espoused, but few know how to apply them on a reliable basis. But enough talk. Let's dance. It's what we do in the water or on land. We are birds, not of the air. Our element is water, even when we describe pirouettes in the sand."

Afterword

And I say the sacred hoop of my people
was one of the many hoops that made one circle,
wide as daylight and as starlight,
and in the center grew one mighty
flowering tree to shelter all the children of
one mother and one father.
~ Black Elk

The experiment known as human beings, a concoction put together by the earth beings and the sky beings, meandered along for eons without coming to any definitive resolution. Neither the earth beings nor the sky beings wanted to give up on them. Their potential for redemption made it easier to tolerate their destructive cycles. There were always some who had the capacity to move through dimensions, to not be trapped on the surface of earth with the other surface dwellers. To move into the underworld or the sky realm, to bring the magic of those dimensions to the surface of earth, so we may begin to understand the multiple possibilities of our existence.

Our ancestors, the sky beings and Earth Mother herself join us with all others in this expanding and contracting universe. The peace of water, the transformation of fire, the pleasure of earth, the muse of air.

*What the caterpillar calls the end,
the rest of the world calls a butterfly.*
~ Lao-tzu

About Atmosphere Press

Atmosphere Press is an independent, full-service publisher for excellent books in all genres and for all audiences. Learn more about what we do at atmospherepress.com.

We encourage you to check out some of Atmosphere's latest releases, which are available at Amazon.com and via order from your local bookstore:

Twisted Silver Spoons, a novel by Karen M. Wicks

Queen of Crows, a novel by S.L. Wilton

The Summer Festival is Murder, a novel by Jill M. Lyon

The Past We Step Into, stories by Richard Scharine

The Museum of an Extinct Race, a novel by Jonathan Hale Rosen

Swimming with the Angels, a novel by Colin Kersey

Island of Dead Gods, a novel by Verena Mahlow

Cloakers, a novel by Alexandra Lapointe

Twins Daze, a novel by Jerry Petersen

Embargo on Hope, a novel by Justin Doyle

Abaddon Illusion, a novel by Lindsey Bakken

Blackland: A Utopian Novel, by Richard A. Jones

The Jesus Nut, a novel by John Prather

The Embers of Tradition, a novel by Chukwudum Okeke

Saints and Martyrs: A Novel, by Aaron Roe

When I Am Ashes, a novel by Amber Rose

Melancholy Vision: A Revolution Series Novel, by L.C. Hamilton

The Recoleta Stories, by Bryon Esmond Butler

About the Author

"Been meditating every day for 50 years. I reckon it's done me some good." So says author Howchi Kilburn, whose quest has led him into soul and spirit, the magical lore of the Ancient Ones. When not writing, he plays with his grandkids and sits in expectation that people can heal themselves. Communities can too, maybe even nations. Gentleness, openness, attunement and peace are our natural way of being. May our presence of Mind help us to attain and sustain the Way.